Can You See Me

CHASING CHAOS DUET
BOOK ONE

D.M. MIDNIGHT

For every bookworm who usually likes books more than people.

For everyone who wants to be seen
and I mean truly seen and accepted for who they are.

Find someone who accepts your chaos and embraces it.

For everyone who wants to find their "yellow", this is for you.

The meaning behind
the color yellow

Your "yellow" is your soulmate or twin flame.
They provide you a safe space to be yourself.
They calm your chaos.
They make you forget about all the negative
and allow you to be unapologetically yourself.
They never judge you and never let you give up.

Playlist

Yellow-Coldplay
Blindside- James Arthur
Tattoo- Loreen
Train Wreck- James Arthur
Safe Place- RuthAnne
Sorry- NF
What's Left of You- Chord Overstreet
butterflies- Isabel LaRosa
I Choose You- Forest Blakk
Perfectly Broken- BANNERS
Empty- Letdown.
Deja Vu- James Arthur
Never Let You Go- James Arthur
Certain Things- James Arthur
Savage- Whethan
Infinity- Jaymes Young
3am- Laszewo
Femme Fatale- Mon Laferte
I Found- Amber Run
Let Me Love the Lonely- James Arthur

Author Note

This is a Dark Romance that contains topics that can be triggering. Please read the following tropes/triggers before making the informed decision to continue. Your mental health is important.

- Emotional Manipulation

- Stalking/Kidnapping

- Murder

- Severe Car Accident

- Gun/knife

- Blood

- Medical abuse/manipulation

- Touch Her/Him and Die

- Morally Grey MMC and FMC

- Obsessive MMC and FMC

- Possessive AntiHero

- Bad Boy/Bad Girl

- Soul Mates

- Amnesia/Broken Memory

- Public Play

- Shared Past

- Kinks: primal play/ knife play

- Identity Change

- Second Chances

- Stalking

- Masked man

Prologue

Atlas

I'm sitting at my desk, swirling the last sip of whiskey in my glass. This is my third glass within the last hour. Something to take the edge off while I brace myself for the storm that is about to hit me. I contemplate refilling my drink again when I finally hear her. I knew this would happen when she found out, I just didn't expect her to be this mad. Her footsteps echo through the house as she storms her way to my office. I don't know how a woman her size walks that loud. There's a clatter and something that sounds a hell of a lot like glass shattering. It's followed by a muttered curse before she's throwing the door open with enough force to knock the picture of us off the wall.

"A fucking TRACKER! Really Atlas? You have that little trust in me that you put a tracker in my phone?"

"That tracker has nothing to do with trust, Maze. You know better than that."

"Right, this is just another one of your stupid power trips. You can't handle the fact that I don't bow to your every command.

I'm not a dog, Atlas. I will not be your pet or some puppet you can play with. You don't get to control me! I'm done! I can't keep playing these games with you."

"Then leave, Maizyn! Control is the only thing I have in this world. I don't need you or your chaos fucking up my life anymore!"

She flinched as if my words had slapped her. Her eyes began to water as she turned around, storming back out the same way she came. I almost took the words back, but I didn't. I wasn't too worried about it. It's not like what I said mattered; she'll come crawling back later, she always does. She just needs some time to cool down. It's not the first time she's been pissed at me, she just likes reacting as chaotically as she possibly can. She will probably call later to apologize for overreacting.

Maizyn

I speed out of his driveway, heading toward the closest bar. I'll show him the chaos he claims me to be.

My entire life has been crazy, that's where I thrive. This would never work out anyways. He is far too controlling for my free spirit.

My ex tried to control everything I did and I refuse to let another man think I'll be a puppet. So I am going to do what I do best... get blackout drunk and decide what to do next.

Pulling into an empty parking spot as I arrive at the bar, I throw the car in park and make my way inside. The bartender must've seen the wild look in my eyes because he started lining up rows of shot glasses before I even reached the counter.

"What's your poison? You look like you're gonna need it."

Slamming Atlas's black Amex onto the bar, "Tequila. Lots of tequila and keep the tab open."

The least he could do was pay to get me drunk.

The bartender keeps trying to make conversation, but I'm not really in the mood for half-assed small talk. My ability to pretend I care disappeared after my third double shot of tequila. At this point, unless he's placing another shot in front of me, I act like he's not even there.

Maybe my self pity and self destruction will be my own demise.

I replay the argument over and over again in my head. He wouldn't tell me why he put the tracker on my phone. If it wasn't about trust, then why wouldn't he tell me the reason?

Whatever.

It's not like his reasoning would even matter. The tracker is there either way, and Atlas made it very clear that I was too much for him.

As I swallowed my eighth shot, a brilliant idea came to me. If Atlas didn't want me ruining his life, then I'll grant him his wish.

I won't come back this time.

We can't keep doing this back and forth. It was never good for either of us.

I pulled my phone out of my back pocket to send a text to Atlas. It's a hell of a lot harder than I thought it would be.

I stare at the screen longer than necessary because I honestly fucking swear, the letters on the keyboard kept moving.

Between the double vision and swirling letters, it takes about twenty minutes for me to type it out. At least, I think I typed it correctly.

Maze: u don't wat me so I wn't bothr u agin

I attempt to hit send and sneak out while the bartender has his back turned. I wasn't closing out my tab, they could keep Atlas's credit card. I didn't want it, and he would just try to track it to find me. Stumbling to my car is an even bigger pain in the ass task to complete. It takes five tries to unlock the car door, but I managed to get it unlocked.

I sink into the driver seat with a big sigh, and attempt to start the car. It's a hassle for sure. It's like I'm looking through a pair of beer goggles.

Thankfully this car was push-to-start, or I wouldn't be leaving this parking lot.

Driving probably isn't the best idea, but why would I care?

It's not like anyone cares about me. Hell... I'm not really sure if I even care about myself.

Peeling away from the bar, I start heading away from town. The further away from him I get, the less likely I'll be tempted to contact him again. It's time to break the cycle.

Atlas will never change and it seems like neither will I. This is the only way forward that my drunken brain can think of.

I get a few miles up the road when I remember about the tracker on my phone. If I keep it he will know where I'm at. Without hesitating for a second longer, I retrieve my phone from my back pocket and launch it out the window.

The crunch of it breaking when it hits the ground is pretty satisfying.

Damn, I'm going to miss my phone.

No social media is going to suck, but cold turkey is the only way to make sure we'll stay out of each other's lives. Eventually I'll need to get a burner phone or something. The kind that's hard to trace. If he wants me back, I'm going to make it as hard as possible on him. I refuse to run back to him this time.

Atlas doesn't always get to win.

My vision continues to get worse the further I drive.

How much did I drink again?

There were too many road lines in front of me to tell which lane was the correct one anymore. Suddenly, the road gets very bumpy, and the car skids to a stop when I hit the bottom of a ditch.

Oops, maybe I am *too* drunk to be driving.

Laughing, I unbuckle my seatbelt and maneuver myself out of the car. Not sure if it's because I'm drunk, but my body feels fine. Nothing hurts as far as I can tell.

The damage to the car doesn't look bad from what I can see, but what do I know. I'm too drunk to even stay on the road. I already forgot that amazing plan I had back at the bar, but it was too late to turn around now.

I'm so fucking stupid.

What the hell is wrong with me?

Why can't I have normal reactions just once in my life?

You know, talking would've been the normal way to deal with this, but I decided I was going to run away!

Fuck it.

He was right, all I do is mess shit up. I will get far away from here one way or another. He has a life, and I don't fit into it. I never did.

He didn't want me. He didn't NEED me.

I won't apologize this time for being who I am.

I was too much for him and I refuse to let anyone clip my wings ever again.

No amount of love was worth diminishing what little light I kept trapped inside my ribs. If they can't handle me at my worst, I refuse to water myself down to be loved. I choose me this time.

If someone else won't pick me, I'll pick myself.

Standing here doing nothing isn't going to get me anywhere. I start to walk, not certain if it's the right direction, but I stopped caring.

I walk for about fourty-five minutes, until I arrive at a little corner store. I have no clue where I was at this point, but I couldn't walk much further.

Stepping inside, I grab a few snacks for the rest of my trip, then walk to the check-out counter to pay for my items.

As she hands me my receipt, I finally get the courage to ask her what I came in to ask.

"Hey... I'm so sorry to bother you, but is there any chance you could call me a taxi? My um car... broke down, just up the road, and I'm just trying to get to a hotel nearby until I can get it fixed."

"Yeah, no worries hun. If you want to sit outside, they should be here in about six minutes."

"Thank you so much! I really appreciate it."

I exhale slowly as I sit on the curb outside waiting for the taxi to arrive. My head is swimming with thoughts that are too fast to grasp.

Where the hell am I going?

What should I do next?

The beep of a horn startles me from my thoughts.

Well shit.

I hope he wasn't waiting too long, I didn't even hear him pull up.

I give the man a sheepish wave, brushing my pants off, before climbing inside.

"Where to, miss?"

With no plan in place and being too drunk to think straight, I retort the first thing that came to mind.

"The first hotel across the state line."

The rest I'll figure out once I sober up. He gives me a quick glance through the review mirror but doesn't comment anything, before putting the car in drive and taking off.

The driver keeps trying to make conversation, but I ignore him. Not to be malicious but, I don't have the energy to put in the effort.

I'm spiraling, I know that.

I can spot the warning signs a mile away by now. Everything is becoming too much again– The emotions, the regret– all of it.

We passed a road sign stating that the state line was five miles away, and my bravado crumbled.

I start reaching for my phone, feeling myself caving. I let out an exaggerated sigh when I remember it's currently laying shattered on the side of the road somewhere.

What a great fucking idea that was. I can't help but roll my eyes at my own stupidity.

Maybe the driver would let me use his phone?

Only one way to find out.

"Hey Sir? Could I possibly use your phone to make a call? I seemed to have left mine, I would make it quick I promise."

He doesn't even hesitate before handing it to me. "Here, no worries take all the time that you need."

I grab it from him and mutter a quick "thanks" before dialing Atlas' number.

The line begins to ring and I hold my breath.

If he answers, I'll turn back around and we can figure it out.

If he doesn't answer, then I'll keep moving forward.

It takes eight rings before I reach his voicemail. I feel my heart shatter just a little bit more. Looks like I made the right choice. In that case, I will at least tell him a proper goodbye. When I hear the beep, it all just pours out. I tell him everything on my mind. I'm halfway through when I hear the sounds of tires screeching. I glance up just in time to see bright lights.

I'm too impaired to comprehend what I'm seeing, but it doesn't take more than a few seconds before impact.

I hear it before I feel it, the sound of metal crashing into metal.

I feel my head ricochet off the window before the car begins to flip and everything goes dark.

Atlas

My phone starts ringing right on schedule, except it's not Maizyn's name flashing on my phone. It's some unknown number, so I ignore it and let it ring until it goes to voicemail. It's probably just a work call.

If it's important they can leave a message, and I'll respond to the call in the morning during business hours.

She left my house three hours ago. Usually on her way back here by now.

Just as I go to see if she texted me, I get a notification from my banking app saying my credit card was used, the one I gave her.

I chuckled to myself as I checked the transaction history.

Lucky's Sports Bar– I should've known. She managed to rack up a $150 tab. That's impressive, even for her.

She was definitely drunk and probably got a ride home. Whatever, if she doesn't come back tonight, she'll be back tomorrow.

It's always the same cycle.

I wasn't going to wait for her.

I had to work in the morning and didn't have time for her weekly drama.

I woke up the next morning to the ringing of my alarm. Still nothing from Maizyn. She's probably still sleeping off a horrible hangover.

I wouldn't be surprised if she slept most of the day, I wasn't going to waste time thinking about it. I go about my normal routine then head into work.

I greet my receptionist as I head into my office. It's not a traditional office, more of a room with an abundance of computer screens. This is my work space. Any meetings I'm forced to take in person are held in the board room down the hall. No one else, other than Gavin, is allowed in here.

I'm filtering through potential job requests to see if anything requires our immediate attention when my phone rings.

"Torres Security, this is Atlas."

"Uh yes, this is Corey. I work down at Lucky's Sports Bar. Um, we just wanted to inform you that we have your credit card here. A woman came in last night and opened a tab with it but she left prior to closing the tab...We are only able to hold it for 24 hours before we have to destroy it."

"Thanks Corey, I'll be there later today to retrieve it."

I exhale as I slam the work phone down. She always had to make shit difficult. She was so drunk, she couldn't even remember to bring my card with her. I fired out a text to her letting her know that she forgot my card, when I noticed the voicemail notification from last night's call that I forgot about. Might as well listen to it now.

I expected it to be work related, someone inquiring about our services. That couldn't have been further from the truth. Maizyn's voice cracked as it came over the speaker.

"Hey Atlas... It's me. I know you don't want me in your life anymore. While that sucks, I will respect that, because you're right. All I ever do is fuck shit up. I make life messy for you and you don't deserve that, so I'm breaking the cycle. I won't come back this time.

All I ever wanted to do was love you but I can't even do that right. So this is..."

Her voice trails off before there is an audible gasp followed by the sound of metal colliding, and glass shattering right before the voice recording ends.

Something in my chest breaks as the phone slips from my hand. I'm frozen in place for a few moments, trying to comprehend what I heard.

Was she driving drunk?

What the fuck happened?

After a few minutes, the shock wears off and I spring into action.

I fire off an SOS text to Gavin and then I call her. The phone doesn't ring, going straight to voicemail meaning it's probably dead or worse.

Gavin storms in with his laptop as I try to think of what to do next. Normally I'm fine under pressure, but something has me shaken.

"What's the SOS, Atlas?"

Before I respond to him I throw the mask back in place. I wasn't about to show my cards to anyone, not even Gavin, until I figured out what really happened. He didn't know about her and I didn't think now was the time to tell him everything.

"We have a high priority job. Missing persons case and it hasn't been long enough for the police to step in, so they hired us."

"Okay, what do we know?"

"Target's name is Maizyn Lewis, 26 year old female. The last known location was Lucky's Sports Bar some time between 11pm and 2am. There was a tracker placed on her phone, but it is currently disabled."

It's possible, with a little bit of work, I could ping the last location but it'll take time."

He studied me for a few seconds before responding, "start trying to locate the last ping on the cell phone, I'll start on the cameras and see if we can find something."

I nod my head at him as I turn towards my screens and begin typing. It didn't take long for Gavin to hack into the CCTV cameras near Lucky's.

"Can you give me a description so I know what I'm looking for?"

"Shit, yeah my bad, long wavy brown hair. Last known wearing blue jeans and black shirt. She should've been driving a black Altima."

It takes a few more minutes before he spins his laptop to face me. "Is this her?"

I turn to see the recording of her getting out of her car and storming into the bar.

"What's the time stamp?" It takes everything in me to keep my emotions in check. I force my voice to stay monotone but it comes out sounding so detached, I barely recognize it.

"11:48pm."

I scribbled that down on the notepad next to me. "Okay, watch and see if you can find what time she left the bar."

"Gotcha." Even though his response was quiet, it was measured, clearly depicting how focused he is on the task at hand.

I lose track of time trying to ping the cell phone location, when Gavin finally speaks up. "Uh. She leaves at 1:16 AM, but you might want to see this."

I glance at his screen and see her stumble her way towards her car.

She is so drunk, she can barely stand up straight. She is definitely too drunk to drive.

Fuck.

Panic arises in my chest as I remember that voicemail, but I shove it back down. Now is not the time to lose my shit.

"Call Kyle and have him put an APB on her car. I should have the last known cell phone location in a few minutes."

As soon as the screen pings the coordinates, I send them to Gavin, and we rush out the door. I'm not familiar with the location so we map it as we climb into my car.

The GPS led us to the side of the road, ten minutes from the bar, but we didn't find her or her car. There was nothing here. It was deserted. Even though we don't see anything, this is still the last known location of her phone. We pull over and start looking around until I spot it, her phone shattered to pieces in the middle of the road. I step closer to the phone, but I already know it's useless. The phone won't give us anything in this condition. I pick it up, putting it in my pocket anyways.

So much for a tracker.

Feeling defeated, we climb back into the car and start heading back towards the office when Gavin's phone pings. He glances at me, looks back at the phone, before his eyes lock on me again.

"Spit it out already. What's the text about?"

"It's from Kyle.. they found the car. It's about twenty-five minutes from here. How she got that far that drunk I have no idea, but do you want to check it out now?"

"Yeah, the faster the better, which way?"

He points back behind us so I pull an illegal U-turn, and continue in that direction. The further we drove, the more anxious I got.

The sound of metal crushing replayed in my head as I imagined what I was going to see when we arrived.

My heart beat sped up as her car came into view. It was definitely in a ditch, but didn't look as bad as I thought it would considering what I heard. I jump out of the vehicle and rush to her car as soon as I put mine in park.

"Alright, Gavin. I'll check the car. Can you check the roads ahead to see if you find anything while I do that?"

"Of course, man. I'll let you know if I find anything."

He jogs ahead as I look in the car. Any amount of hope I had vanishes when I find that her keys are still in the ignition, and her belongings are still in the car. Everything she always brings with her is here, but she is nowhere to be found.

Where the fuck can she be?

There isn't anything here to make me assume she was injured. Not a single trace of blood can be found. Snapping my head in each direction, I look for any signs of her.

Nothing.

It's a dead end.

While I'm glad I didn't find her laying in the fucking ditch or bleeding out somewhere, that doesn't ease my mind. There aren't even footprints leading away from the car.

Gavin runs back to me, placing his hand on my shoulder. "Atlas, I think it's time we head back to the office and try to find out more. There's nothing we can do here, there are no leads."

While it pains me to agree, I know he is right. I let my silence say everything that I currently can't. No matter how bad I want to keep looking, we have no leads, so I agree and we head back to the office.

The only thing left to do was to call hospitals to see if she was at any of them. I called twelve hospitals. Fucking twelve, and every single hospital said the same thing.

She wasn't there. Twelve different calls just to be told that she wasn't at any of them.

There's no way she can just vanish. She has to be somewhere, so I hacked into the city cameras trying to find any trace of her. I was able to code in an alert that would ping my phone anytime facial recognition came across someone fitting her description.

Before I noticed, the sun had gone down and was currently rising again. She had officially been gone for over 24-hours and the longer it took to find her, the worse I felt. I wouldn't give up until I found her.

All the files on my desk blur together at this point. I know what they all say. I could probably recite the papers word for word without even looking at them. It doesn't matter how many times I reread them, they still won't lead me to her.

I run my hands over my face before tugging at my hair in frustration. There has to be something I missed.

Suddenly, I remember the voicemail didn't come from her number.

Whose phone did she call from?

I scramble for my phone I threw across the room earlier in anger. I click on the voicemail, calling the number. On the sixth ring, a woman's voice came on the phone. "We won't be taking any calls while we're mourning our loss," then the line disconnects.

My phone fell from my grasp.

My thoughts start to spiral, making it difficult to keep up with them.

She said mourning.

Maze used this phone and now they are mourning someone.

Is that what happened to her?

When she said she was leaving, I thought she meant me, not this world.

It felt like I was just shot in the heart. I can't breathe, my ears ringing. I clutch my chest as I try to squeeze the pieces back together, but it was no use. All I manage to do is bloody my hands as I watch the sharp fractures fall through my fingers and scatter to the floor at my feet.

My vision goes blurry and I panic when I can no longer see anything in front of me. I think I'm going blind until warm droplets run down my cheeks, and realize I'm crying... I didn't know I could even do that.

I didn't know what to do.

I want to tell Maze I was sorry for everything.

She was the only good thing in my life... I know that now.

Chapter One

Atlas

It's Saturday night and we're relaxing in our usual spot. The VIP booth at Elixers is dark enough we won't be bothered, but it gives us a full view of everyone else in the room. I won't sit with my back to a room, EVER. It could just be me being paranoid, but I like to think it's the fact I can never turn my hacker brain off. Not everything my company is hired to hack into is exactly legal, but as long as the money keeps flowing in, I do what I'm best at without asking questions. It's not like it can be traced back to me anyway, so I don't really care.

Gavin is already looking for his next victim. Some chick he'll sleep with and string along for a few weeks before ghosting her. It never fails. He shoots me a cocky wink, walking off towards two blondes standing by the bar. I chug what's left of my whiskey and prepare to head home. Scanning my surroundings one last time before I leave, I stop as soon as I meet a pair of dark green eyes from across the room.

Those eyes are attached to a five-foot-three brunette whose hair tumbles past her shoulders in waves. I've never seen her in this club before and, while I didn't particularly feel like dealing with people tonight, there's something captivating about her.

Unlike other women in this bar wearing dresses that barely cover anything, she stands in the middle of the crowd wearing black jean shorts, fishnets, a crop top, and black converse. She carries herself like she owns everything she does without a care in the world.

Before I had time to plot out my next move, she was walking towards me. I swear the air changes temperature with each step she takes. I can't help but follow her with my eyes. The way her hips sway as she walks, her eyes darkened with mischief.

When she stops in front of my booth, the temperature drops ten degrees. The tension between us is thick enough to cut with a knife.

The way she raises her brow as a smile twitches on her lips told me everything I needed to know. She's looking for trouble, that much is obvious.

The question is, will I let her drag me into it?

She parts her lips and I brace myself for the cheesy line women always spew. But surprisingly, what comes out of those plump lips is the complete opposite.

"Is there something I can help you with, Mr. Business man? You seem to have a problem keeping your eyes to yourself. Am I too underdressed for you that I'm ruining your night? What's the deal?"

To say I was shocked would be an understatement, but I couldn't let her know that.

I motioned for the bartender to send over another whiskey. I was going to need a drink for this one.

"You're mistaken, Darling. I didn't notice you until you were standing in front of me, but since you're already bothering me, you might as well have a seat and make it worth the disruption."

She huffs out a breath but scoots into the booth opposite of me anyways. A wicked smirk reaches her lips as soon as my drink hits the table. Her eyes flick to my drink twice before she locks eyes with me again. This is about to take an interesting turn, I can already tell.

"Whiskey? May I try it?"

I slide the glass towards her without saying a word and watch as she takes a sip. She doesn't make the slightest face as she swallows it. A woman who can drink whiskey and she drank it like it was water. That more than got my attention.

She wasn't like anyone I've ever met before and that irritated me, for the simple reason that I didn't know her name yet.

Well, fuck. This might become a problem.

She, in fact, seemed to have some kind of effect on me and I didn't like it one bit.

"It's good... Just good, sadly. Though, I know what would make it taste better, but I'm not sure if you're up for it."

"Try me."

With my whiskey glass still in her hand, she quickly rounds the booth to stand next to me. I angle my body towards her as she reaches for my chin with her free hand. She puts one foot on the bench behind me, and my hand automatically wraps around her upper thigh to steady her.

What kind of game is she playing and why am I enjoying it so much?

She tips my chin up until I'm staring back at her. There's that smirk again.

What the fuck is she about to do?

"Open your mouth."

She taps her index finger against my lips until I comply. I thought she was going to pour the whiskey into my mouth, but no, that would've been too easy.

Nope, she takes a sip and instead of swallowing it, she spits it into my mouth before pushing it closed. Her lips brush against mine before I can react to what she just did.

Beep! Beep! Beep!

Beep! Beep! Beep!

Beep! Beep! Beep!

My eyes flutter open and reality settles back in.

Of course it was another fucking dream.

It's been five days and I've relived five different memories. I fucked up and now she's gone. Maybe just from my life, or maybe, from this world entirely. She'll probably haunt me in my dreams until the day I die.

I deserve it.

I shouldn't have let her walk out the door that night. I have no idea what happened, I can't find a single trace of her, like she vanished into thin air.

No matter how many cameras I hack or how many leads I try to follow, I can't find her. I keep replaying the voicemail she left me. The weight in my chest gets heavier every time I hear her voice break right before the loud sound of wreckage.

No one knows how much she means to me. At the time I even refused to admit it to myself, so no one knows how much this hurts me. They have absolutely no idea how much I'm crumbling under this mask I put on every morning.

It's morbid, but I check the obituary section on the news website again like I do every morning, praying I never come across her.

If I don't see her name next to a picture of those blazing green eyes, then it gives me hope she might still be out there somewhere.

When I don't come across her name, I get up and continue the cycle. I've always prided myself on being organized. I want everything to work efficiently. It didn't always bore me, but it works.

I will live a boring life, if it means I get to control the outcome.

My friends and company depend on me to keep a tight ship. I, for one, prefer having a meticulous schedule. Wake-up, work out, go to work, sleep, my routine visits to the club on Tuesday and Saturday nights, then repeat.

It leaves little room for error or surprises. Errors? I can fix, but I don't do surprises. Surprises seem like organized chaos I have no control over.

I thrive in situations I can control.

He who has control, has all the power.

I went into tech, knowing full well that I didn't have to deal with people face to face. And when I do, it's usually transactional, something good for business and nothing more. I refuse to pretend to care when I don't. Emotions aren't really a thing I do, I've protected my mask of indifference for a long time.

My father taught me at a young age that emotions were useless. They make people weak. While I may hate my father, I agree with him on this. Emotions are messy, I don't have time for messes in my life.

At least that's what I thought, until her.

My need for control was one of the main reasons I started Torres Security, with the help of my best friend Gavin. We practically grew up together, and he's the only person I trust to never betray me.

It took Gavin years to break through my walls. He's like a brother more than anything else. No one else is even close to knowing the real me, just him and Maze. But, I had to fuck it up and push her away.

How fucking stupid can I be?!

I keep to my routine like everything is normal. To the outside world, it is.

No one, not even Gavin, has noticed my well-placed mask, but day by day I feel the mask cracking.

I'm not sure what feels worse; being numb or feeling EVERYTHING.

Before she came into my life, I was numb. Everything was a dull grey and I simply went through the motions.

I was just a mask among many others.

I knew the faces I needed to make to match what I should've been feeling, but that doesn't mean I felt them, my father made sure of that.

I knew my thoughts and actions weren't exactly normal, but there wasn't much I could do to change that.

The day I met her....how could I ever forget that day?

It was the first time I felt my own heart beat, and it fucking scared me. It skipped in my chest. I thought I was dying.

I wish I could flip that switch in my brain controlling my emotions and turn them off, but I think she broke it the day she stormed into my life.

I don't know how much longer I can keep pretending.

I also didn't know what I was going to do if I didn't find something soon.

Chapter Two

Atlas

I've been looking forward to this day for a while now.

As the wedding procession begins to play, I watch my fiancé walk down the aisle in a modern style white satin slip dress. The only reason I know the type of dress is because it's all she talked about for weeks.

She's beautiful.

Her chestnut hair has streaks of caramel when the sun hits it just right.

The normal wavy strands are twisted into an updo.

This is probably the most dressed up I've ever seen her, but even on a day like today her vibrant, emerald eyes still swirl with pandemonium. I vow to myself to never let that chaos die out.

There's a weird pressure in my chest when she smiles at me, but I brush it off. I clasp her hand in mine when she meets me at the end of the aisle.

The officiant says something I don't hear.

She has my full attention.

I can't take my eyes off her.

My eyes keep moving over her, trying to memorize every single detail of this moment.

I can't believe this woman agreed to marry me. Her hand gently caresses my cheek causing the world to rush back in around us. I give her a sheepish smile before finally turning my attention to the officiant.

We take turns reciting our vows, then the officiant says the iconic line, "You may now kiss the bride!"

My hands wrap around her waist as we both lean in and, right before our lips touch, my eyes snapped open and my heart shatters all over again.

Reality always crashes in when I'm awake.

That dream was new.

Instead of a memory, it was a future I'll never get. I'll never get to kiss my bride.

It's been four weeks since I last saw her and it's pretty clear that I'll only be happy again if I'm asleep.

I still haven't told anyone about her.

As far as Gavin knows, she was just a job we couldn't crack. I also know if I tell my mother what happened, she would probably think less of me because she raised me better than to treat women how I treated Maizyn.

Unfortunately, the longer I sat in my thoughts, the more lost I felt.

When I met her, it was the first time in my entire life I knew what emotions felt like. Happiness felt a lot better than feeling nothing. I felt warm and giddy around her.

Can you believe that... my black icy soul felt warm.

It no longer felt like I was living in shades of grey.

She gave my life color and meaning.

Those small glimpses of happiness she blessed me with will continue to haunt me because I was fucking stupid and took it for granted.

I thought I would have more of it– more time, more her.

I didn't think I'd lose my yellow....I didn't think I'd lose her.

I didn't know what I thought I'd accomplish by brushing her off and letting her leave. But I do know one thing, if I could go back and rewrite our story, I already know what I'd change.

I wouldn't have let her walk out the door that day. I'd have told her the truth. I would explain the reason for the tracker, and I'd spend every free second of my time soaking up the love she tried to give me.

Now that I'm without her, I wish I was lucky enough to feel numb. Being numb would be a fucking blessing right now. I thought this fight would blow over and she would be back later that day.

I couldn't do this shit anymore.

I needed to tell someone before I drove myself crazy.

So I do the only logical thing I can think of.

I caved and called my mother.

Even though I didn't want her judgement, she'd know what to do next. She's the most level-headed person I know.

"Hey MaMa, I need some advice..."

"What happened, hun? Why do you sound sad, is everything okay?"

I spent the next thirty minutes going over the details. I tell her everything.

From how Maizyn and I met– everything in between– up to how I let her leave that day. My voice cracked as I explained the voicemail I received. My words scrape my throat on the way up as I tell my mother I couldn't find her anywhere.

"Aw, sweetheart! I'm so sorry. I imagine you're so heartbroken right now."

Heartbreak is a funny thing... It's strong enough to be a physical feeling. It felt like I was shot in the heart.

A bitter chuckle slips out. "Yeah mom, imagine finding out you have a heart the moment you feel it shatter into a million pieces. I don't know if I can stay here much longer, everything reminds me of her."

"You could always come stay with me, son. I still have your room made up just the way you left it. Have you talked to Gavin about it yet?"

"While I appreciate the offer, I'm going to decline. I have to do this on my own. I'm too old to run home to mommy just because I'm hurting. Also no, you're currently the only person who knows."

"You know you have to tell him, sweetheart. If you're going to leave town, you at least have to tell him why."

"You're right mom, I'll talk to him. I'll let you go so I can have him swing by."

"Okay sweetie, you know my offer still stands, if you need it."

"Thanks, Mom."

I end the call, then text Gavin.

> Atlas: Hey man, if you have time, can you swing by? I got some shit I need to talk to you about.

> Gavin: Yeah. I can be there in half an hour.

The minutes seem to tick by slowly as I try to figure out how to tell Gavin I lied about Maizyn. I also have to figure out how to tell him I need to leave.

I've never lied to him before, I never had a reason to. We don't tell each other about the women that we see unless we think it's serious.

Gavin, on one hand, has never been a serious relationship guy. He jumps from one girl to the next without remembering their names. I, on the other hand, wasn't much better. I avoided most women. It wasn't worth the hassle when my hand could get the job done perfectly fine.

Well, Until her.

The only problem is, the fact that I didn't know how serious it was with her until she was gone. I ultimately had to lose her, to know the difference.

My thoughts are interrupted by a knock at the door. Knowing it's Gavin I go to let him in.

I don't say anything when I open the door, just gesture for him to follow me. While he knows this is an odd behavior for me, he doesn't say anything. He follows me into the living room and plops down on the couch. Instead of joining him I remain standing, locked in thought.

"Atlas man, what's up? Why did you ask me to come here?"

"Look I...fuck." I start off, pacing the length of the room before handing him my phone. "Just listen to the last voicemail on my phone. We can start from there."

He takes the phone from me and listens to the voicemail. I know he heard the wreck when his eyes flick to me and he grips my phone tighter.

"Atlas what the fuck did I just hear? Who the fuck was that, and why is it on your phone?"

"That was Maizyn Lewis. She...she meant a lot to me and I fucked it all up. That night we had a fight. In short, I told her I didn't need her in my life, so she left and went to that bar. It's not the first argument we've had. I didn't think anything of it until I heard that voicemail. It's some random number, so I didn't answer it that night.

I figured whatever it was, I could deal with it in the morning. If I would've answered, maybe she wouldn't be missing right now. I... I told her I didn't need her and it's like she fucking disappeared. She could be dead and I wouldn't fucking know!"

My composure cracks a little further with each passing second.

"Man, just sit down and we can figure it out."

I sigh but plop down next to him.

"It sounds like this is important to you. Why didn't you ever tell me about her? How long were you two seeing each other?"

"I met her like six or seven months ago, at Elixirs actually. You left the bar with some chick right before she came over to me. I planned to tell you, if it became something real. I didn't understand how important she was until it was too late. At that point, I didn't realize she was the one for me. I completely ruined it, and I was embarrassed to tell you, or anyone for that matter."

"What else are you not telling me Atlas? I know that look."

"I can't stay here Gavin. This house, this city, it all reminds me of her. Until I figure out what happened, I can't be here."

"If you're leaving, I'm coming with you man. We can find a little office space and relocate Torres Security for the time being or let Ramos run shit here while we're gone. We can start looking for places now."

"I didn't ask you to drop everything and move your life around for me."

"You didn't have to. So, where're we going?"

"I haven't figured that part out yet."

We spend the next hour scouting out possible office locations, when I come across one that captures my interest.

"I found one in the next state over, about three hours from here. Close enough to the main office that we can get here if anything goes wrong. I sent you the listing. Can you get it taken care of while I search for housing options close to it?"

"Okay. I'll look at it. Also, don't worry about looking for a house. I'll reach out to a realtor to see if the company has any houses in the area. That way we only have to deal with one company for both properties."

"Yeah, that's smart."

A few minutes go by before Gavin says, "I emailed the realtor now and sent an offer worth more than the listing price. I'll let you know when it goes through. Do you need anything else taken care of on my end?"

"You're good to go. Can you let Ramos know the plans? And uh, thanks. You don't have to come with me. Just because I can't stay doesn't mean you have to leave too."

"Yeah, I got you. I'll text you later with all the details, plus I'm sure Ramos will be happy with the promotion." He chuckles softly.

As he walks out the door, he throws over his shoulder, "You're my brother. Of course I'm going with you. Who else will keep your ass out of trouble?"

I just laugh as he slams the door behind him. I don't know what I'd do without him.

Chapter Three

Emily

Do you ever question reality?

Do you ever wonder if everything around you is real?

Lately, I have doubted everything around me. What I see. What I hear. I doubt every decision and step I make. At this point, do I even really exist?

Everything seems too much– My feelings– I either feel too much, or nothing at all. Colors were too bright, sounds were too loud, and my skin felt too tight. My thoughts ping ponged off the walls of my brain.

I'm not sure if I'm sane or a maniac.

What if I'm a ghost? Maybe I just need a therapist, but then again, if I AM real, it would only add character to my already charming personality.

It's very possible that I'm just finally losing my mind, but I can't even remember the last time I talked to someone who wasn't myself.

Well, myself or Trevor.

He's been by my side since I woke up in the hospital. Other than him, it's almost as if people don't see me. They walk past without acknowledging me, like I'm translucent, invisible to the world around me.

Last week, someone bumped into me and acted like it didn't happen. Hence, why I'm starting to believe I'm either a ghost, or a figment of my own imagination. How cool would that be, to think yourself into existence?

It doesn't help that I have no memory of how I got to the hospital, or why I was actually there.

Maybe I died and I'm simply roaming the Earth.

It would make a great story.

If only it were true.

I continue my path down the over crowded sidewalk while I try to make sure I'm only talking to myself inside of my head, and not out loud.

If I'm real and people CAN see me, I'd rather them not know I talk to myself, or hear the type of conversation that I have. They'd probably think I was on drugs or something.

You know, I never liked how busy this part of the city is. It makes me feel weird. Somewhere between my skin itching, and wanting to throw up.

I don't really do people well. If that makes sense? It always feels forced or like I'm pulling teeth. I think it's probably just anxiety but, who has time for that?

I start thinking about what I can remember about my life.

I vividly remember my mother telling me I had an overactive imagination growing up, that could be why I feel this way. I can hear her southern drawl in my head, "Emily, I swear the only friends you make are them fictional ones you read bout in these books." She never said it with heat or anger. I don't even think she meant it in a bad way.

I was always antisocial, an introvert. I preferred burying my nose in a book over hanging out with people who added very little substance or meaning to my life.

What was the point of pretending to be someone I wasn't?

They would just talk about me the moment I left the room, so why would I waste time and energy, yet still never be good enough?

Kids in school were mean, there's no reason to put attention on myself if I could fly under the radar instead. Given my current situation, it would've been nice to have at least one friend.

Having someone that'll always be there for you sounds pretty nice. While the conversations I have with myself are riveting, it gets lonely sometimes. Trevor tries, but it always feels forced around him.

I have a lot of blanks in my memory recently. I woke up in a hospital bed and Trevor was just sitting there. It's all very confusing. He claimed the hospital called him to pick me up because my surgery was finished. I don't remember having surgery, but my foot was in a boot so I tried to piece the clues together.

He keeps telling me everything's fine, and the doctor told him it was a possible side effect of the anesthesia. I couldn't think of a reason not to believe him, so I went along with it. What reason would he have to lie about that? I have memories of us together, so I know he isn't lying about that part.

Something still feels off though.

I get this nagging feeling that I'm forgetting something very important. I just wish I knew what's going on. I'm missing about a year's worth of events, and no one but me knows that.

I honestly just pretend I remember whatever events Trevor talks about, hoping my memories come back soon. I feel less like myself each day that they don't. It feels like my soul is displaced.

When I first woke up, Trevor would seem tense or angry every time I asked about what happened. He, in fact, showed me medical files that corroborate his story. Based on the paperwork, doctors had to surgically repair my ankle, but it didn't say why. The doctor wouldn't tell me and neither would Trevor.

He'd brush off my concern like I was being childish, like my feelings were invalid. So I stopped asking. I'm not sure what he's hiding or why, but I have enough shit to worry about.

I was so preoccupied with my monologue I didn't even realize how far I walked– or limped would be more accurate– until I smelled that familiar scent.

There was this cute little coffee shop nestled into the corner of the shopping plaza. You could smell the ground coffee beans and the sweet smell of fresh baked blueberry muffins. Those were to die for.

Honestly, anything Mrs. Carter made was delicious. It also happened to be the place I started working at after I was cleared by my doctor to work again. Mrs. Carter was the only person who ever acknowledged me. I also find it funny we have the same last name even though I'm pretty sure we're not related. She still treats me as if I'm her granddaughter, and would want to talk if I went inside to order something.

While I love her dearly, I wasn't in a people mood today. It's my day off anyways and she'd probably scold me again for coming in when I should enjoy my time off. I didn't have the heart to tell her, her shop was one of the only two places in this world that allowed me to breathe normally. Instead of going in, I walked past the little blue shop and stepped into the door next to it.

I exhale a breath I didn't realize I was holding the moment the bell on the door chimes above my head. This place feels more like home than anywhere else, and Mrs. Carter's bakery was a close second. I come here every time I need a break.

When my thoughts get too heavy, this is the only place that makes me feel better. Something about the smell of books makes my soul feel lighter. I've been coming to Pages at least once a week for the last two months. I stumbled upon this gem of a hidden bookstore after one of my shifts, and now every time I visit this place, I don't want to leave.

Life has been hard lately.

I've been hiding from Trevor, trying to avoid him when I can. He acts the way a loving boyfriend would, but it doesn't feel real. It feels like he's putting on a show. Shit, if I'm being completely honest, I was running from myself too.

I was trying to outrun the thoughts in my head. I'm missing too many memories and can't figure out why. The panic attacks started two days after I got released. Every time I try to piece the missing parts of my life together, it happens, the panic takes over.

I'm not saying this place cured me, because it hasn't. All I'm saying is my mind is a little nicer to me when it's confined in these four walls.

It gave me a PLACE to run to when I didn't have SOMEONE to run to.

It's the one place in this world where the quiet doesn't seem so silent. My own thoughts can't take over when the books and pages whisper to me, they always have. If I could live here I probably would.

Books have always been my safe place.

They don't judge me like people do.

Like I judge myself.

It's always a good kind of silence here.

As I walk to my normal spot in the darkened corner, I notice something about today feels different. For some reason, I decided to stop mid-step and listen, like I would be able to hear what was different today. But the only sounds I can hear are the pages turning in a book, the scratch of a pen gliding across paper, and the clacking of computer keys.

Huh, it sounded the same as every other time... what could it be? Damn, maybe I'm finally going crazy. I press play on my imaginary pause button and resume my trot to my favorite spot.

While this corner of this book store isn't much to most people, it's sometimes the ONLY thing to me. It has become my safe spot. The owner said as long as I didn't disturb anyone, I could make this my little space.

It's cozy, decked out with a beanbag chair on a SUPER fuzzy carpet, with a small table. I have a cute reading lamp, and a cup of highlighters and pens, so I can annotate any of the books I end up buying or reading here.

It's not like I own this corner, but the regulars know this is my spot and tend to leave it alone. Maybe I should put up a velvet rope so no one'll bother my space.

The moment I plop onto the big bean bag chair, the warning bells go off in my head. I freeze, something not feeling right. I can't quite name it, but the feeling is there.

Someone's been in my spot I'm sure of it. I don't know why something like this rattles me. I inhale deeply to calm my nerves, but it has the opposite effect.

There's a smell that's different than when I normally sit here. It's woodsy and sweet, kind of like oranges and... clove? Is that even a normal scent combination? Is it a candle? Air freshener? Cleaning supplies? None of those options seem right.

Then it hit me. What if it's someone's cologne or perfume?

My eyes dart around for any other signs someone has desecrated my sacred spot. *I know I'm being dramatic– Shoot me.*

My eyes flick from the lamp, to the rug, back to the lamp again. Everything seemed fine, that is, until my eyes landed on my cup of pens. I snatch the cup off the table and dump them on the floor and, as I suspected, my favorite pen is missing.

So someone *has* been here. Great.

I take some calming breaths coming to the conclusion, someone sitting in my spot isn't the end of the world. Like I said earlier, I don't actually own the spot. Maybe this spot is a safe place for someone else as well. If this spot can help someone else feel a little less crazy, then who am I to stop them.

I would like to have my pen back though.

The odd thing about this entire situation isn't someone sitting here, it's the fact the scent makes my brain feel fuzzy. I'm not sure why, but I know this scent. I can't pin down the memory, but I'm not a stranger to the feeling it provokes. It feels safe.

Chapter Four

Atlas

If someone would've told me a year ago I'd move away from my hometown, I would laugh. The control freak in me doesn't like change. Who knew that it's my control- or lack of control- that would have me packing up and expanding the business.

If it wasn't for Gavin, none of this would've been possible.

He dealt with my salty ass the whole time we worked on this move and got settled. If I'm being honest, he did all the heavy lifting. He had to deal with the realtors and all the paperwork that came along with this move.

And I? I was just trying to survive.

I still check the online obituaries, still no sign of Maizyn. I guess no answer is better than finding out she's dead. The dreams don't happen as often anymore either. They only happen maybe once a week now, usually one of the many amazing memories of us together. While she still sits at the back of my mind, I'm no longer actively trying to find her. I have to try and move on. If she was alive and wanted to be found, I would've found her already. I just hope wherever she is, she's okay.

Not only was this fresh start good for me, it's good for the company.

Two different locations allow us access to more jobs, which in turn, brings in more money. Ramos is loving his promotion so I don't have to worry about the Allendale office while we're setting up this one. It took awhile, but it's finally starting to feel normal here. I wouldn't call it home, but I don't feel out of place either.

I haven't explored much of this new town yet, but I did find this book store on my way to get lunch last week that caught my attention. I'm unsure why but I went inside to check it out. It was cozy, and there was a reading area set up in the corner. It felt homey and made me think of Maze. Since then, every time I'm in the area I stop inside.

Today is one of those days.

Entering the bookstore, I walk straight to the beanbag in the corner and plop down. This spot has become a safe space. A place to just relax for a few minutes. I take a moment to soak in my surroundings, Maze would've loved this place. I can't help but feel closer to her while sitting here. I never end up staying long, but it helps nonetheless.

I walk out of the book store and as I turn to head back to work, I collide with someone.

My instincts take over as I steady the person I bulldozed. The hair on the back of my neck stands, and my skin prickles where we touch. Only one person has ever caused this reaction, so when I glance down and meet the familiar green eyes staring back at me, I freeze.

Emily

My skin jolts with electric shocks.

I'm hyper aware of the place where his fingers grip my arm. I feel the heat travel from his hand, up to my warming pink cheeks.

Great, I probably look stupid.

One quick glance at his eyes feels like he can see my very soul. His eyes flash with the kind of recognition I can't decipher, and I instantly panic. Without giving him any time to insult me or say anything rude, I storm off.

Of course my limp decides it wants to be extra prominent at this moment. I huff out a sigh of annoyance as I brush the invisible lint from my clothes. Anything to distract myself from turning back around. So embarrassing. I'm so lost in my own head that I collide with a stranger.

I've got to stop talking to myself and spacing out. Yet, I keep wracking my brain to find the shit I can't remember.

I rush into the coffee shop and clock in.

After placing my items in my locker, I relieve Brooke from her post behind the register and get to work. I can't believe I ran into someone. If I would just act fucking normal I would've seen him coming out of the book store instead of colliding with the man.

I can still feel where he touched me, my tummy warming with butterflies. I don't do butterflies, never have. What makes him different?

Something at the back of the line catches my attention, so I reach up on my tippy toes to peak over the person in front of me. Imagine my surprise when I notice that the mystery man I collided with while I tried to enter the bookstore just a few minutes ago, is currently in line.

I take a few orders from the customers before him, preparing myself to face him before he approaches the counter. *Just my luck, he probably followed me inside to probably yell at me.* The closer he gets to the counter, the more my hands start to sweat. I can't exactly hide from him either. Brooke doesn't like to work the register unless she has to.

He finally gets up to the counter, but instead of yelling, he doesn't say anything. He stares at me like he's looking at a ghost. The silence becomes awkward so I decide to speak first.

"Hey, sorry sir for bumping into you. I should've been paying more attention, and I should've apologized when it happened. My bad."

He blinks a few times like he didn't expect me to speak. It takes a few more minutes before he responds.

"So you've been here the whole time and didn't have the decency to tell me?" The words are bitter in my ears.

I physically feel my face pale. That's not what I expected him to say at all.

"What are you talking about, why would I tell you? I don't even know you."

That seemed to trigger him. Anger flashed in his eyes as he clenched his fist before he covered it back up.

"Real fucking funny, Maze," he hisses. "The joke is over. Cut the shit."

I flinch at his tone but recover quickly.

"I...you must be mistaken. I'm not sure who you are, and I definitely don't know anyone named Maze. My name is Emily. Also, I'm pretty sure I would remember if I met someone like you."

He glances down to my name tag and back to my eyes. He must see the confusion swirling behind them because the next thing out of his mouth is an apology.

"Sorry."

He parts his lips like he's going to say more , but it dies on his tongue. Nothing about this interaction is going how I thought it would. His brow furrows before he finally speaks again.

"I um, I guess I made a mistake. You just happen to look a lot like someone I used to know. I apologize for any inconvenience."

"Oh. Okay. Did you want to order something or...?"

"Shit, my bad. Can I just get a double espresso?"

I quickly make his drink and cash him out. After handing him his espresso, he gives me one last glance before walking off. I was hoping he'd leave but instead, he sits down at a table in the corner and drinks his coffee. I can't help but to keep glancing his way.

Something about him is intriguing.

I've never shown interest in anyone.

Why do my eyes keep flicking back to him?

It's almost like my eyes are magnetized to him. He hasn't reacted to my lingering eyes. He either doesn't notice or doesn't care. Not really sure which option I'm hoping for. It's like he casted a spell on my psyche.

I try to go about my regular task while he's here, and I feel like I'm doing an okay job until he stands to leave. I'm hyper aware of his movements as he walks over to the trash can to throw away his empty cup.

The bell of the door chimes signaling him walking out, and it feels as if there's a sharp tug in my chest. Like a rope is connecting us, and the further he walks, the harder the tug gets. And I have no idea why. Before I have time to think too much about it, I yank off my apron and yell over my shoulder that I'm going on break. My feet carry me out the door and I head the same direction he just walked off in.

Instead of running to catch up to him, I stay at a steady pace with a few people behind him. I'm not sure where we're going, but it feels like it'll be fun to find out.

Shit!

Why the fuck am I following him?

What the fuck is happening to me?

I don't do this!

I don't even like people, so what makes him so different? My brain is so disrespectful sometimes. This shit makes me look crazier than I already thought I was.

Maybe I should start looking into finding a therapist.

Do you tell your therapist you started stalking a person because he looked at you, and you felt seen for the first time in your life? Do they report illegal activities?

Yeah, maybe I should keep this to myself.

I can picture it now: laying on a couch in a stuffy room, the judgemental lady tapping a pen on a clipboard, asking me what brought me in. As soon as I trauma dump on her and tell her that I can't remember shit from the last six months, she will look at me like I'm crazy.

Can you imagine her face when I conveniently tell her I have somehow become a full-blown stalker. When she asks me why, I can proudly tell her it's because someone I accidentally bumped into, had looked at me and made me feel fuzzy. Pretty sure that'll be the exact moment she realizes I should be shipped off to a padded room and never let me go.

I swear my brain is becoming my worst enemy, lately. I can no longer tell the difference between finding my mind or losing it.

How do you know if you're even good at stalking?

I really wish they made "Stalking for Dummies." That's a book I need.

What if he sees me and realizes that I'm stalking him?

Will he think I want to hurt him?

That's kind of laughable with my five-foot-two-inch stature.

I'm tiny compared to his height. He's definitely over six foot, maybe six-foot-three.

Will he find me charming and endearing?

Will he call the cops?

Shit.

That's definitely not what I need.

I don't want to be handcuffed, thrown in the back of a cop car, and be treated like a criminal. I'm not a criminal, it's just some light stalking. I just want to know everything about him before he knows anything about me.

That seems like a perfectly normal reaction to me.

If I don't think too hard about it, I won't overthink what I'm doing.

I follow him for the next two blocks until he enters an office building. *Interesting*. I wouldn't have pegged him as the boring office type, but I'll bite.

Once I believe he's far enough inside that I won't be caught red-handed, I sneak over to the plaque beside the door that lists the address for the building, as well as what businesses this building holds.

There are only three listed.

Suite A is something called Nailz. I'm assuming it's a nail spa. Suite B is a photography studio of some sort. It's the last Suite that piques my interest. Suite C is a place called Torres Security. Somehow I just know that's where the mystery man went. I quickly type that information into the notes app on my phone and rush back to work.

Chapter Five

Atlas

I storm into my office, immediately pacing the length of the wall.

Those green eyes were unmistakable.

I blink and they're all I can see in my head.

Either I'm hallucinating, or she's a fucking liar.

I'm leaning more towards the latter. There are too many similarities between the two women for it to be anything other than deception.

FUCK!

I flip my office table before I even realize I did it. At least it wasn't my desk with the computer monitors on it. Papers and security contracts flutter all over my office floor, but I don't feel any better.

My anger still simmers underneath my skin.

I thought I was coping fine with her being gone, with the possibility that she's dead. This move was supposed to be a fresh start. Is it possible that I'm more fucked up about it than I thought?

Am I finally losing it, or is it really her?

My dreams always feel so real, but my brain has never tricked me while I was awake. I have to get to the bottom of this.

I flop down in my computer chair, pulling up the city CCTV on my computer screen. I need to know my mind isn't playing tricks on me. I pull up the camera right outside the book store, scrolling back to about an hour ago, and watch from there.

After twenty minutes of watching the playback, I pause the video as she comes across the screen. I slow down the frame rate and click play again, watching until I come out of the bookstore and walk right into her. I replay the same five minute clip on a loop, trying to catch anything I didn't see the first time. The camera angle doesn't give anything away, not even a good view of her face. I didn't notice any cameras inside the coffee shop that could be hacked into; therefore, that wouldn't be an option.

I pull out my phone and text the only person who'd know how to help me.

Atlas: I think I'm losing it, man.

Gavin: What happened?

Atlas: I bumped into someone on the street today and everything in my body is screaming that it was Maizyn.

Gavin: That's a bad thing? You wanted to find her right?

Atlas: Of course I wanted to find her. That's not the problem.

Gavin: Alright, what is the problem?

Atlas: I confronted her and she looked at me like I was crazy. She said she didn't know who Maze was, that her name was Emily. She said she didn't know me.

Gavin: Are you sure it was Maizyn?

Atlas: Fuck man, I thought I was, but the more I think about it the less confident I am. She genuinely looked confused. What do I do, man?

Gavin: Let me look into it for you. It probably wasn't her, so try and relax. Send me any info you have on Emily and let me do what I do best.

Atlas: Sure. Her first name is Emily and she works at Mrs. Carter's Bakery, over on Third Street in the West Plaza. I will email you the surveillance video I got from outside the bookstore. It doesn't show a good angle of her face, but it's all I was able to get.

Gavin: Send it to me and I'll get back to you when I have the information. Take care, man.

I hate that I keep bothering Gavin with my mess but I know I can always count on him. There's no way I'll be able to get any work done until I get answers, so I pocket my phone and head home.

I can clean my office up later, right now, I need to clear my head.

Emily

I make it back to the bakery in time for our lunch rush to hit. We have a line out the door when I arrive, so I rush inside and put my apron back on. I jump back behind the register, allowing Brooke to focus on making the drinks.

With how busy we are, time flies by. Megan comes in shortly to replace me, and I don't stay longer than I need to. My mind is itching to do some digging on that mystery man I met earlier. It doesn't take long for me to clock out and head home.

It's pretty warm out, but I honestly enjoy the walk. It gives me time to be alone to think, and I always carry a knife with me so I'm not too worried about how safe walking alone in this city is.

My mind keeps drifting back to that man from earlier.

Why did he call me Maze?

He really thought he knew me, but I can't remember ever meeting him, and my name isn't Maze. My body has never reacted to anyone the way it did with him though. The way he looked at me like he held all the answers to every question I had.

I felt like I was missing something. Like there were parts of a puzzle I didn't have and I can only assume my missing memories were the reason for that feeling. I have to find out who this man is and why he looked at me the way he did. I have to get my memories back.

I round the corner to my apartment building, racing up three flights of stairs to my apartment. This place really needed to invest in an elevator but at least all the steps made my ass look great.

Slamming the door behind me, I double check I locked it, then head to the kitchen island where my laptop sits. I pull up the notes app on my phone to see the business name again. After typing Torres Security into the search engine, I hit enter. The first two results don't give me anything worth noting, but the third result brings me to the company website. I go to the "about us" page and low and behold, a photo of my mystery man shows he owns the company.

Turns out, his name is Atlas Torres and he runs it with another man named Gavin Blackwell. It seems the office here in Willowhook is not the only location they have. There is another location in Allendale about three hours from here, not too far past the state line. Interesting.

I've heard of Allendale before. But where?

I keep digging through the company site, but the only thing I learn is they do all kinds of security jobs. I searched for the name Atlas Torres instead. This man is either super boring or super smart. There's nothing personal I can find on the internet. Even his social media pages look like they're for business only, not even the name of his favorite restaurant can be found.

I decide to search for anything I can find on Gavin. They seem close, maybe that's my ticket to more information. I scroll past a few unrelated profiles before coming across his personal social media account. The last picture was posted a month ago in Allendale, where their other office is.

Based on that information, they're probably new in town. The company site said this branch opened about a month ago, so that tracks.

I keep scrolling for anything that I can use when I see a picture of Gavin and Atlas at some place called Elixirs. I realize they're close, more than just business partners, but it doesn't help me learn anything about what they do in this town.

Fine, I'll do this the hard way. All I have to do is follow him without getting caught. How hard could it be? People in books stalk someone all the time.

With that, I come to a simple conclusion, I now have a long day ahead of me tomorrow. That means, I need to get ready for bed in order to wake up early enough for this.

On my way to the bathroom, I grab an oversized shirt from my dresser. Reaching inside the shower, I turn the handle all the way hot before I start to undress. I washed my hair yesterday and I'm too lazy to deal with it tonight, so I pull it up in a messy bun while stepping into the shower.

I welcome the way the hot water burns my skin. When it comes to showers, I want the Devil himself to flinch. I grab the loofah, applying some of my Lavender body wash to it. The scratch of the loofah against my sensitive skin while I lather my body with soap is so relaxing. I use a scent free face scrub to exfoliate quickly before washing it back off.

I know I should shut off the water and get out, but I'm not ready yet.

While I'm secluded in this tiny square I'm hoping my brain will finally be able to shut down for a few seconds. I just want to forget everything that's happening outside of this shower while I'm in it.

But of course, it doesn't really work. It never does.

The universe will never allow my thoughts to be quiet. Instead of shutting all the voices out, they amplify. Trevor's voice every time he tells me what I should and shouldn't do. The nagging weight of my self doubts. And then there is him, the mystery man.

Sighing, I close my eyes, imagining his blue ones staring back at me. If I couldn't make my mind turn off, then maybe I could use it to my advantage. I instantly drop the loofah and allow my fingers to trail over the suds I have yet to wash off.

What if it were his hands on me instead of my own?

The thought has me opening my eyes in a panic.

Where the fuck did that come from? I was trying to think happy thoughts but not that kind.

I quickly wash the soap off and shut off the water.

The man is a complete stranger. I shouldn't be thinking about how his hands should feel on my body. I do a half-assed job of drying off my body before slipping my shirt over my head and climbing into bed.

Maybe sleep would fix me but I wasn't hopeful.

I set my alarm for 6:30AM. I'm not thrilled about the time, but I need to wake up early enough to hopefully beat him to his office.

Atlas

My phone pings with a text notification. It's two in the morning, so I'm pretty sure it's Gavin. Not many people would send something this late in the night. I'm hoping he found something to confirm my suspicions.

I know what I saw.

I just need proof so I don't sound like I'm losing my mind. I open the text thread, and sure enough it's from Gavin, but my stomach sinks when I read it.

Gavin: I checked. And I don't think it's possible that this girl is Maze.

Atlas: What do you mean?

Gavin: Her identity checks out. Her full name is Emily Nicole Carter. She's twenty four. She doesn't seem to have much family left. All I could find was that her mother died about five years ago.

Atlas: Is it possible it's a cover story?

Gavin: I don't think so. It's pretty extensive. I can track almost her whole life story up until about a year ago. I was able to find that she's on a lease for an apartment with someone named Trevor Sinclair, and based on her social media page, that seems to be her long term boyfriend. I'm sorry man, I was hoping you were right. We'll find Maze. We just have to keep looking.

Atlas: It's okay. Thank you for looking for me. Can you still email everything you found just so I have it?

Gavin: Yeah I'll email everything over to you.

The email doesn't take long to arrive in my inbox. I trust Gavin, but I know my mind won't settle until I look over the proof for myself.

A part of me is hoping he got it wrong, even though that's usually never the case with him.

I open the files as soon as they're done downloading to my computer. Opening the email, I immediately realize how detailed of a background check he ran on her. *Shit, he was busy.* That man is a different type of genius. I don't know how he pulled this much information in such a short amount of time.

Gavin sent me everything I needed to know, right from her birth certificate, to her current job at Mrs. Carter's Bakery. I start looking over everything, trying to find anything he may have missed.

I'm still hoping there'll be something in here showing it's a cover up and this woman is Maze. I'm meticulously looking over every single piece of information he sent me. I read over every tiny detail repeatedly but, I don't find anything to prove she's Maze.

The identity looks as real as it gets. I know from experience as a private investigator, no one would go this in depth on a cover story. The only thing that flags any interest is that almost a year's worth of information is missing, like she took time away from the world before resurfacing again. No listings of a job or housing, but there could be plenty of reasons for that.

She could've been living at her boyfriend's house and didn't have to work. I've seen it happen. When I ran into this woman, everything in my body was screaming she was Maizyn. But no matter how many times I scour over the facts, the conclusion remains the same. It's not her, and while I'm disappointed that it's not, there's nothing I can do about that.

I check the time on my computer and realize it's already four in the morning.

Tomorrow is going to suck. I need to be at work by eight o'clock, and with my current lack of sleep, it'll seem to drag on longer than normal.

Chapter Six

Emily

Morning is here before I know it, my alarm blaring way too fucking loud for six in the morning. I quickly turn it off and climb out of bed, tripping over the blankets wrapped around my legs. I don't remember the last time I willingly woke up this early for anything. My brain refuses to function correctly until at least nine in the morning, and that's being generous with at least one cup of coffee. That's another reason I know I'm already screwed when it comes to Atlas.

The fact that I'm interested enough to wake up this early means it's pushing more along the lines of obsession. Let's not even add in the fact I'm only up this early so I can stalk him. But I got it completely under control. There's absolutely no need for a therapist. I'm perfectly sane. Stalking someone is a completely normal reaction to my feelings, nothing to see here.

I throw on a pair of black sweat pants and a matching hoodie. Today's going to be a long day, so I might as well dress as comfortably as possible. I quickly throw my hair up into a messy bun as I head into the bathroom to brush my teeth. There's no point in dressing up. It's not like he's going to see me.

That would defeat the purpose of stalking. Slipping on my black sneakers, I grab my phone and keys then head out the door. This is a smaller town, so his office isn't too far from where I live, it should only take me fifteen minutes to walk there.

Nothing unexpected happens on my walk. The sidewalks are mostly empty at this hour. I only pass a few people who are heading to school or into work. It's almost peaceful. I round the corner and continue towards Atlas' office. I checked the company website for the hours of operations, so I know they don't open to customers until 8:30am but I have no idea what time employees, or the boss I should say, arrive to work.

As I approach the building, I'm relieved I don't see any cars parked here yet. I'm hoping that means I beat him here. I pull my hood over my head and walk over to sit at the bus stop across from his office building. I figured if I hide in plain sight I'll draw less attention to myself. Plenty of people dressed like me sit and wait for the bus all the time.

I plop down on the bus stop bench a little too hard and hit my elbow in the process. Note to self, hitting your funny bone doesn't feel funny. The tingling pain in my arm finally starts to fade when I notice my first mistake. I scowl at my offending feet. Can I never do anything gracefully? I couldn't even manage to put two matching shoes on my feet this morning. It would've taken me only a few seconds to double check I had matching shoes on.

It's honestly laughable.

I walked around with mismatched sneakers, yet not a single person noticed me. It only adds to the ever growing pit in my stomach that tells me I'm invisible. I almost wish I was a ghost. That'd at least explain a lot of things and I would feel less empty. All this stalking will probably be pointless.

There's no way someone like Atlas would ever have an interest in someone like me. I'm scared I might be too broken for most people. I'm not that delusional. I know whatever I think is going on between us won't lead to anything, but I still can't help myself.

Well I guess I could end up in jail, or a nice padded room if I get caught, whatever, it would be worth it. I may not know much about that man but, there's something undeniable about him. I can't put my finger on it, not sure if I ever will, but something about this man calls to me. Running into him the other day altered my brain. He looked me in the eyes for three seconds, and it was the most seen I've felt in my entire life.

I pulled my phone out to check the time and noticed my inner ramblings lasted for almost an hour. At least time flies when you're slightly manic. Talking to myself makes me feel better though. I start to get slightly antsy when a car finally pulls up. It's a black Audi RS6. I jot down the plate number, in case I ever need it. The car pulls around to the side of the office building and parks towards the back of the lot. I'm hoping that means they work in one of the offices, the only thing I can do is wait to see who comes out. After a few minutes, a man gets out of the car, but it's not Atlas.

This man is similar in height to him though. The hair cut is a similar style but instead of black hair like Atlas, his is chestnut brown. When he gets closer to the main door I'm able to get a better look. I watch him a little longer and I recognize him as the man Atlas works with. I scroll back through my notes app to look for his name. It was Gavin. As he opens the door to walk inside, another car drives past. Gavin throws an arm up in acknowledgment before closing the door behind him.

My attention shifts to follow the vehicle as it parks next to the RS6. This one's also black, but it was a Supra. I've always wanted to drive one of those. The windows are tinted too dark to see inside. This has to be Atlas, but I wait just to make sure. I glance at the time on my phone to make a note of it, 7:45am.

They don't arrive until almost opening time. That's good to know, that means I can sleep in a little longer tomorrow before I head over here. Maybe with a little bit more sleep, I can remember to make sure my freaking shoes match.

He's unmistakable when he finally climbs out of the car, my heart skipping a beat when he comes into view. His messy black hair is long enough on top to fall into his eyes. The sides tapered around his ears, and the back is almost as long as the top. Speaking of his eyes, they're an odd mix between pure blue and gunmetal blue. I haven't been able to get the color of his eyes out of my head since yesterday.

They're mesmerizing, almost hypnotic.

He's dressed in a fitted white dress shirt and black slacks. You can see the faint outline of some of his tattoos when the sun hits his shirt just right. I have to wipe my mouth because I swear I'm currently drooling over this man. I'm not shallow, but that man is yummy. I can't help but watch his every step as he makes his way inside. Thankfully, he doesn't notice me sitting here and vanishes behind the main doors.

My stomach growls. Right, I might need some food if I plan to be at this all day. I need to be able to plan better if I want to keep at this. Books make stalking sound easy, I either suck at this or books lie. I leave my spot long enough to get a coffee and bagel for breakfast before coming back to my recon spot.

This may be boring but I needed to figure out his schedule, and the only way to do that is to sit here all day and follow him. I didn't have the right skill set to hack his phone or anything like that. I had no other way to track him. I should've brought a book with me to give myself something to do while I was here. If I wasn't worried about draining my phone battery I would read an ebook on my phone. I'll get a portable charger next time.

I keep an eye on the entrance as people come and go. Everyone seems like other workers or clients. I don't notice anything worth making a note of. Nothing seems out of the ordinary. Some people sit next to me on the bench as they wait for buses to pick them up, it's all pretty repetitive. No one bothers me or asks me questions. Hell, they act like I'm not even here. That's fine though, it works out better for me that way.

It's right around noon when I spot Atlas walking out of the building. I hide my face the best I can to make sure he doesn't spot me. Once he's a comfortable distance away, I stand and follow after him. He walks with purpose, carrying himself with a confidence I admire. If I walked like he did, would I still be invisible?

We walk for almost a block before he stops in his tracks, making me also stumble to a stop. Can he feel me watching him? Does he already know that I'm stalking him? He starts glancing left to right and I panic. I quickly dash behind a trash can before he's able to turn around. My heartbeat pounds in my ears as I wait for him to find me hiding here.

This is not my brightest idea. What was I thinking? I'm not cut out to be a stalker. I wait for my heart rate to return to normal before I peek out from my hiding spot. He's gone, he must've kept walking. At least he didn't notice me. I take off in the direction I think he headed.

Hopefully I can figure out where he went. I would hate to have wasted my morning just to end up with almost no intel. I have to know everything there is to know about him. It's twisted, but I fear if I don't, I'll always feel hollow. He makes me feel alive without even knowing it.

I get to the next intersection with no luck. I don't see him anywhere. He must've gone into one of the shops I passed. I turn, walking back in the direction I came from. This time I take my time and glance into the shop windows as I pass them. I pass a Cuban sandwich shop, stopping in my tracks. I spot him at the counter placing an order. I jot the information in my notes as I head a little further down the sidewalk and lean against the brick wall outside the candle shop. I pretend to play on my phone while watching out of the corner of my eye for him to leave.

Fifteen minutes later, he starts making his way back to his office with his lunch in his hand. I maintain a further distance than earlier when I follow him back, hoping not to trigger him to my presence this time. The trip back is uneventful. Once we arrive at his office building and he walks in, I continue walking to get a sandwich from the diner one road over. Next time I decide to tail him all day, I'll pack my own snacks so I don't have to spend unnecessary time getting food.

Atlas

Running into Emily the other day is making me paranoid. From the moment I stepped out of my car this morning, it felt like someone's been watching me. Thanks to the connections Ramos and Gavin made over the years, I know we've acquired some clients that dabble in not so legal activities. I usually focus on the more legal clients, but business is business at the end of the day. I really hope we didn't piss off the wrong people. I would hate for my job to be what takes me out. I'm not even sure if I have eyes tracking me, but if I do, that's the only logical reason I can think of.

Other than the constant sensation of my skin crawling with the feeling of being watched, I thought I saw Maizyn again. It was a fleeting glance in the reflection of a store window when I was picking up lunch, but when I turned around no one was there.

Even after all this time, that woman still haunts my mind. It's almost like my nightmares follow me into the waking world.

I know she's not here, but my heart is still trying to convince me otherwise. I moved here to get away from her and all her memories, but the ghost of her seems to follow me wherever I go. I didn't know you could be haunted by heartbreak. It almost makes me want to laugh. I told her I didn't need her, and now I can't seem to function properly without her. The irony is suffocating.

I'll regret letting her leave for the rest of my life. If it continues like this, it won't end well. If I keep letting my guilt fester beneath my skin, I know it'll slowly eat away at what little bit of a soul I have left. Hope and guilt have been at battle for a while now, but I don't know if I have enough hope left to save myself. No one ever tells you your own guilt has the power to kill you.

I spend the rest of my work day completing mundane tasks. It takes me a few hours to go over our current surveillance contracts. I double check that all the required signatures are on them before they can be uploaded into the database for us to schedule the system installments.

Our company does pretty much everything involving security. We install surveillance systems, work events, and even a bit of private investigator work. That's not including any off the record task Gavin or Ramos work on. We try to be all inclusive and, between the three of us, someone has the skills to complete the job discreetly. After confirming all our installs are scheduled and contracts are correct, I open the company email to see if we have any request for PI work or security detail. Most of the inquiries are standard.

People want a few men to run safety measures at local events, nothing new there. I add the events to our calendar and schedule the men needed for each task. Unfortunately for me, I was usually the one stuck doing all these boring tasks. The others preferred to be more hands on and while that was fun, someone had to do all the admin paperwork.

The work day is finally over and I can't wait to get home at this point. I head to my car and the feeling of being watched returns. My eyes dart around taking in my surroundings, but I don't spot anything out of the ordinary. There are several people leaving work and an uber driver picking someone up, but no one seems to be actively watching me. I look over my shoulder one last time before opening the car door and sliding into the driver seat. Exhaling loudly, I crack my neck before cranking the car. I check my surroundings one last time before reversing out of the parking spot and heading home.

Emily

My second mistake makes itself known around five o'clock. I just now realized how shitty my plan was. How am I going to figure out where Atlas lives? I walked here. I can't exactly walk after his car and keep up with him. They really need to make a book called "Stalking for Dummies 101," because I definitely needed it. I was so focused on the overall picture, I forgot about all the tiny important details. I thought about my options for a few moments, trying to formulate a plan quickly.

I didn't have much time before Atlas would probably be leaving the office. I could come back tomorrow after my shift at the bakery and follow him home, but I didn't really want to wait. That only left me with one choice. I pulled out my phone and ordered a ride share. I just hoped they would go along with my crazy idea. The app says my driver, Katie, is only ten minutes away.

Fingers crossed they get here before Atlas leaves. I should've planned better. Winging it makes me nervous and my entire plan is riding on this driver going along with it. I'm hoping the fact she's a woman will work in my favor. The car arrives, pulling up to the curb in front of me. Here goes nothing.

The driver rolls down the window, assessing me before asking, "car for Emily Carter?"

"Uhh, yeah that's me. Look, this might sound crazy but I really need a favor."

"Okay... You have my attention. What do you need?"

"I think my boyfriend is cheating on me, and I want to follow him home from work to see where he goes, but he'd spot my car immediately. Any chance I could convince you to follow his car when he leaves to see where he goes? I can pay you extra for your time."

"Girl, you don't have to pay me any extra, I'm down. This sounds like a lot of fun. Go ahead and hop in the back and tell me more."

I climb in the back seat and point out his car. Just as she opens her mouth to ask for more details, I see him walk out of the main door. "See that man in the white dress shirt walking down the steps right now? That's him."

"Damn girl! I was about to ask what man would be worth the hassle, but never mind. I completely understand just by looking at him. If my man looked anything like that, I think I'd be a little crazy too."

I can feel the blush rising to my cheeks as I nod my head. If she only knew the real story, she'd already know how crazy that man makes me. You can't exactly tell your rideshare you need help stalking a practical stranger just to feed your rapidly growing obsession. I don't think they'd take that lightly. They'd probably lock the doors and call the cops on you, so the lie will have to work.

We watch him walk to his car and I slouch lower in my seat when I notice him looking around. I really hope he doesn't spot me. I don't plan to ever have to explain my actions, that would just be embarrassing. We sit in silence as he climbs into his car and backs out of the parking spot. The moment he shifts into drive, we do as well. She waits until he's a few car lengths ahead before pulling away from the curb and following after him.

"Have you ever tailed a car before? You seem to know what you're doing."

She laughs, "No, this is the first time I've followed someone. I've seen people do it in movies and I've always wanted to try, so thank you for the crazy opportunity. This is pretty exciting. I thought today was going to be boring. The people around here like their routine."

"Well I'm happy I could make work fun for you. I appreciate you doing this. I didn't really have another option. I'm not sure what I would have done if you told me no."

I take my phone out again, making sure I take detailed notes of the road names and what turns we take. It might be useful to know what route he takes home, just in case I ever need it. I really hope he's going home. I'd hate to be following him to his actual girlfriend's house, if he has one.

Shit. I didn't even consider that being an option.

He could be married or something, and I was stalking him without a second thought about it. Would I stop if he was? I'm not proud to say it, but probably not. The fixation on him runs too deep for that to be possible. I'm truly fucked when it comes to this man. I always thought I may be slightly crazy, I never thought I could be psychotic. I guess you learn something new about yourself every day.

If I ever did see a therapist, they would have a field day trying to fix all of my issues. I didn't even understand all of my issues. I lean forward to crank up the radio. I don't really feel like talking anymore. Katie shoots me a glance, not saying anything. She must notice I'm lost to the thoughts swirling in my head.

Atlas hits his breaks and pulls into a drive way. We slow to a stop a few houses away not to draw too much attention to ourselves. Looking around, I take note of anything that may be important for later, but nothing really stands out. I type the address into my notes but everything else looks normal. It's a cozy little neighborhood that looks like every other one in this tiny town. I don't see any other cars here, so hopefully that means he lives alone.

I watch him type in a code to get into the front door. I should've expected the guy who runs a security company to have a system installed on his own home.

I can already spot one camera from here, so there were probably several others. It would be naive to think he doesn't have a fancy doorbell that has a camera on it.

That eliminates any chance of me getting out of this car for a closer look. Going anywhere near his house would likely get me caught on camera. If he has cameras, then it'd be unlikely I would be able to get inside without tripping an alarm.

I'm about to ask Katie if she can bring me back to the bus stop when a familiar car drives past, pulling into the same exact driveway Atlas is parked in. It only takes me a few seconds before the clues click together, and I pinpoint who that car belongs to. That's the car Gavin was driving earlier. Do they live together? Is he just stopping by?

Holy shit! What if they're together?

This could complicate everything. I watch as Gavin exits the car and goes around the side of the house, entering a code to unlock the back gate. Now I'm really confused. I need more answers and I don't think I'll get them today. I sigh in defeat and turn my attention to Katie who's already watching me. She's probably trying to gauge my reaction, but I refuse to give her one. She seemed like a nice person, but I didn't trust her enough to let her watch me lose control.

"Can you please just take me back to the bus stop. I think I have done enough recon for the day. I appreciate your time."

"Yeah, no problem. Are you sure you don't want me to take you home?"

"No, it's fine. I prefer to walk home. It'll give me time to clear my head and sort my thoughts."

"Okay, really sorry you didn't find what you were looking for."

I nod my head, not saying anything else as I turn to look out the window. The drive back is short. It feels a lot shorter than the drive to where Atlas lives. I know that's not really possible, but it's probably due to the fact I'm trapped with my thoughts again. I open the car door as soon as she shifts into park. Before I'm able to shut the door, she stops me.

"Hey. Before you go, I wanted to give you my phone number. Just in case you ever need someone to help you with another situation like this one. I'll always be down to help a girl out."

I quietly handed her my phone. She put her number in my contacts, texting herself before handing it back. Taking the phone back from her, I turn and walk away. It's been a long day and I know I barely scratch the surface on figuring that man out. I'm in way over my head, but there's no way I can give up now. I knew Atlas and Gavin were close, but how close are they? Am I barking up the wrong tree and wasting my time? Do I care either way?

Chapter Seven

Emily

I questioned my sanity a little more each day. If I wasn't working or at the book shop, then I magically appeared wherever he was. I never thought about it anymore; it was subconscious at this point.

Thoughts of him invaded my every waking moment. If i didn't have eyes on him, then he was on my mind. It felt more like compulsion than a choice. My feet always carried me to him without even trying. It felt as if my soul was tethered to his, and the rope attached between us would pull me towards him against my will.

I'm not saying I didn't want to watch him and learn everything there was to learn, just I no longer had the choice to stop even if I wanted to. My obsession with this man was starting to control my life and I did absolutely nothing to attempt to stop it. This obsession with him has become a living, breathing thing, and I fucking bowed to it like it was my master. What does that say about me?

What does it mean for me to be this obsessed with a man I only met once? Simply for the fact it felt like he looked at me and really saw me, instead of looking through me like everyone else always does. Am I really that broken? I know this isn't healthy but, this is the least fractured my mind has felt in years. Maybe it's the opposite though. Maybe I *am* too far gone.

If the voice that's always screaming at me to be heard finally took over, then I truly am losing it. I've spent years trying to keep it locked away. I pushed it down over and over again because I was told she wanted too much. Every time she has ever been allowed to lead, we've ended up broken. Every time someone said we were too much, we fractured a little more.

I'm so tired of being invisible, of making myself smaller to be accepted. Maybe a psychotic break is what I need to pick up all the scattered pieces and stitch them back together. What if that voice was right all along?

The further my obsession pulls me, the harder it becomes to ditch Trevor. It doesn't matter how many times I brush him off, he keeps showing back up. He's persistent, sure and yes, I know I'm supposed to be his girlfriend, but he's not Atlas. Trevor is nice and cares a lot about me. He says he loves me, but he doesn't make me feel anything close to what I've felt in the few seconds I had with Atlas. Trevor also refuses to talk about my missing memories. He says it's for my safety and he's just doing what he thinks is best for me, but I know he's keeping secrets. I wish he'd take the hint and just leave me alone.

The more time I spend sneaking off to be with Atlas, the more Trevor seems to show up and push boundaries I've tried to put in place. He never fucking listens. He keeps brushing everything I say aside like nothing I say matters. He makes me feel like I don't matter. Every time I ask about the events that led me to being in the hospital, or why I can't remember things, it gets worse. He's resorted to ignoring me completely when I bring it up. He'll ignore me like I'm a ghost, or like I don't exist until it benefits him.

Take today for example. I wanted to do some more research on Gavin because of his connection to Atlas, and I needed to stock up on groceries and other things for my apartment. I can't really do research with Trevor there, and as far as the store goes he refused to let me go by myself. He showed up randomly this morning and pushed past me when I opened the door, like he belonged here. In a way, I guess he did.

His name was on the lease, but I didn't want to be near him. I told him I was leaving to head to the store, hoping he'd take the hint and leave, but instead, he insisted he needed a few items as well and would drive me there. As infuriating as it is, there isn't much I'm able to do about it. I'm pretty sure he got the hint but chose to ignore it. He doesn't seem to care much about what I want, so I'm not surprised.

I no longer like being stuck in a car with him. It feels like there are too many secrets between us. I just hope that whatever he's keeping from me is small in comparison to what I'm actively trying to keep hidden from him. It's pretty hard to have a secret bigger than stalking a man while you have a boyfriend, or whatever Trevor is to me at this point. Our entire ride to the store is masked in silence. It's awkward and heavy, but neither of us attempts to break it. Turning my head towards the window, I watch as the buildings pass by. It would be peaceful if I wasn't trapped in this car with him.

The ride is uneventful until his hand suddenly lands on my knee. My body flinches involuntarily. I hope he didn't notice my reaction because the last thing I want to do, is try to explain myself to him.

I tell myself it's because I wasn't expecting the touch, but in truth lately, his touch has been making me feel sick to my stomach. It feels wrong and makes me want to crawl out of my own skin.

Any attention from Trevor feels like a betrayal to the man I only met once. There's also a nagging feeling at the back of my mind that my body knows something my mind no longer does. I don't push his hand away, the last thing I need is for him to question my reaction and focus more of his unwanted attention on me.

As soon as the truck is in park, I open the door and head in the store. I didn't want him near me so if he refused to respect that, I wasn't going to make it easy for him. I grab a shopping cart, rushing to the back of the store. I wanted time to myself before I had to deal with his annoying presence again. I go through each aisle, grabbing anything that looks interesting. I should really start planning meals. I always end up with mismatched ingredients that don't go together to make a meal and I always wait until my fridge is completely empty before I go to the store to restock. I'm pretty sure my meals yesterday consisted of pepperoni and trail mix. Not very filling or healthy, sadly.

As I reach for a bag of chips, something in my peripheral stops me in my tracks. Maybe the better word would be someone. I catch sight of a tall man with familiar black hair. I abandon the chips on the shelf, letting my feet carry me towards the same pull I can never resist. I walk past a few aisles with no sight of him. Did I imagine him being here? The heat rushing beneath my skin tells me there's no way this was my imagination. I almost give up looking when I finally spot him.

He was dressed in simply black jeans and a white t-shirt. He looked very different dressed like this compared to the dress clothes he was in when we first met, or the clothes he usually wears to work. He almost looked hotter this way. The dress clothes look amazing, don't get me wrong, but seeing him in jeans just hits different. He looks more relaxed dressed this way. Don't even get me started on the way his arms look when I finally see the tattoos that cover them.

His entire right arm is covered. I can't tell what each one is from this far away, but it's captivating. Something about the way each design swirls together to create a cohesive sleeve makes me want to trace each one. Black ink peaks under the sleeve of his left arm, hinting at more artwork. I wonder how many tattoos he has. I'd give anything to see all of it. This man is mouth watering, and unfortunately my mouth isn't the only set of lips he makes drool. This man has too much control over my body without even knowing it.

It's really not fair that this stranger has such a strong hold over me. I lose all control over my own body anytime that he's around, and he doesn't even know it. We're strangers, yet I'm drawn to him like it's fate. I peak around the corner of the soda aisle so I can continue to watch Atlas as he walks to the checkout line.

"What the hell are you doing, Emily?"

I jump from his voice, spinning around to face Trevor. Fuck! I completely forgot he was here with me. I have to start being aware of my surroundings. It's becoming pretty clear I make a shit stalker, but it's like every time I'm around Atlas my brain malfunctions.

"Nothing, let's just go."

His eyes flick towards the direction I was looking, but he doesn't say anything before grabbing my arm and pulling me into the opposite direction. I really hope he didn't see too much. I'm not sure how he'd react to finding out about Atlas.

Atlas

The feeling of being watched continuously follows me around. It's not all the time, but it's often enough to be concerning. I have no idea who'd be keeping tabs on me. I check with Gavin, and as far as he knows, we haven't accidentally made any enemies, so that eliminates that option. It's starting to get to me. I don't like not having control over the situation. There were too many unanswered questions and unknown variables.

I'm at the grocery store when the hairs on the back of my neck stand up again. My skin warms, and I already know whoever it is has to be the same person that's been watching me. My body reacts the same way every time.

While I don't like the idea of being watched, I can't help but be intrigued by the way my body reacts to it. It's different. I glance around while trying not to be obvious about it. I don't want to tip off whoever it is. I don't want them knowing I'm on to them. If I'm going to catch them, I don't want them to see me coming.

I feel the eyes follow me as I make my way to the check out area. I really want to know the motive. They haven't seemed to try anything to harm me, but that doesn't mean they won't try to eventually. I couldn't think of any men I've interacted with lately that would have a reason to stalk me. I needed to talk to Gavin about this. I needed to figure this out before this person decided to escalate the situation. I didn't need them catching me by surprise.

As I begin scanning my items, I hear a commotion behind me. I can't make out the words but, from where I'm standing, I hear what sounds like a man's angry voice growling something with venom. I snap my head in the direction it came from and catch a glimpse of a man about 6'2 with blonde hair, pulling a woman down the soda aisle in the opposite direction. He's average looking. Nothing I see is worth noting until my eyes land on the woman he's pulling behind him.

I can't see her face from this angle, but my heart skips a beat in my chest. The hair and height immediately make me think it's

Maizyn. I look away and shake my head, clearing my vision. I know it's not possible for her to be here, but I see her everywhere lately. I turn back to confirm what I saw but they're gone. I think I'm slowly losing my mind. I look for her everywhere I go. I need to get to the bottom of this stalker and learn how to move on. I rush through bagging my items and cashing out. I can't wait anymore. I need to take action now if I ever want to move past this. Maizyn Is gone, I know that. I just need to stop my stalker and get over it. I text Gavin as soon as I finish paying.

Atlas: I got another favor to ask. You got time to discuss it?

Gavin: You know I'll always have your back. How can I help?

Atlas: Can you open a secured text thread?

Gavin: Yeah, give me one second.

Gavin: Okay. The line is secure. What's going on Atlas?

Atlas: This may sound crazy but I think someone is stalking me. I keep feeling like I'm being watched, but I can never figure out who it is.

Gavin: I guess that explains your weird question about enemies the other day. When did you first notice it?

Atlas: It started right after I ran into Emily and had you look her up. So I'm starting to think whoever he is, he's connected to her.

Gavin: That's possible I'll look into it.

Atlas: Thanks. Just let me know whatever you find out.

Gavin: Of course, man. Just be careful.

Atlas: I will be.

I really hope he finds something. The last thing I need is to be caught off guard by whoever has been following me around. I need to know what they want, so I can plan accordingly. It's bad enough I lost Maizyn. Now I have a stalker to deal with. Will I ever catch a break?

Chapter Eight

Emily

Trevor has been around way more than I would've liked. Luckily for me, he's supposed to be out of town for the weekend helping his brother with something, so I finally have time to myself. I've spent the last few days trying to find out anything I can on Gavin.

With Trevor hovering all the time, I haven't been able to, until now. I've barely had any time to follow Atlas this week. I really wish I knew how to hack cameras, it would've made this so much easier.

I don't plan to stalk Gavin, he's of no interest to me, but he's an important part of Atlas' life, so it'll be beneficial to do my research. I start by doing a google maps search of the house they share. The aerial image shows what most people would call a mother-in-law suite in the back yard.

I'm assuming this is where Gavin was going the other day when I tailed Atlas home. That makes me worry a little less about them being more than childhood friends. I'm pretty sure I let my imagination run wild with that one. I knew they were close so I'm not sure why I panicked.

Doing some digging on Gavin has its perks though. He has more of a social media presence than Atlas does, so I'm able to get an insight of some of the activities they do together and places in town they frequent. I take plenty of notes of the locations and times they seem to visit these places. Any detail that helps create an accurate schedule for Atlas. I want to know where I can find him any given time or day. It also allows me to see a few candid photos of Atlas, and a few selfies of the men together.

Atlas always seems so grumpy in every photo, it's kind of funny. Gavin is definitely more carefree out of the two. Atlas seems like he prefers to be in control of the situation and like he'd rather do anything else than socialize. I save any pictures that have Atlas in them. I may need them one day, who knows? This might end up being the only way I'm able to see him, if I'm ever caught for stalking.

Atlas

The feeling of being watched has been less frequent this week, but it's still there. I've been taking notes of the times and locations where that feeling returns. If I can pinpoint the when and where, I'm hoping Gavin can use the cameras to find out who happens to be here with me in each scenario. I need to find the pattern and put an end to it. I still haven't been able to spot the man following me. That's concerning, given the fact I run a security business. I have to be missing something. I can't figure out a motive and have absolutely no idea of anyone who'd do this.

My life isn't that interesting. It's been over a week since Gavin started helping me, but he hasn't figured it out either. There doesn't seem to be a man around consistently unless there's more than one person watching me. Something in my gut tells me it's one person though. I can't explain how I know, other than the fact the air feels charged the same way each time. I also don't know why this started just after running into Emily.

Is the stalker connected to her or is it a coincidence? What am I missing? I'm heading to the bookstore when I feel it again. It starts at the base of my neck and the chills spread across my body as my blood begins to heat like it always does. Why does my body react this way to being watched by whoever this person is? I slow my steps but don't turn around. I want to drag this out as long as I can, hoping we can catch something this time. Without drawing more attention to myself, I swiftly send a text to Gavin.

Atlas: Heading to Pages, the bookstore right next to the bakery, Now.

Gavin: On it.

Atlas: Let me know if you find anything.

Gavin: No suspicious men in the area.

Atlas: Shit, I thought we had them this time. There are not many places someone could hide on this road.

Gavin: Sorry man. Look, I have an idea that might work.

Atlas: I'm listening

Gavin: I'm going to run all the footage through a program that'll flag anyone who is shown in more than one video. Maybe we need to broaden our search with this one Atlas. We have no idea who this person is, or if they are even a man at this point.

Atlas: Do whatever you need to do and keep me posted.

Gavin: You got it.

I continue on my way to Pages. I know Maizyn isn't here, but I need to be as close to her as possible and, in this city, it's there. I know she's never been there, but I know she would have loved it. She always preferred any place where books were found even though I never knew why. Maybe if I ever see her again, I'll ask her. She never seemed to do anything without a reason, even in her most chaotic moments. I enter the book store and immediately make my way to the cozy beanbag I always find myself in.

It's where I feel Maizyn the most.

Sitting here for just a few moments allows the guilt to not feel so heavy for just a little bit. I stick my hand into my pocket to pull my phone out, when my fingers brush against something else. The paper crinkles in my grasp as I retrieve it. It looks to be a crumpled up note. I didn't put this there, so it must be from my stalker. When I open it I can't help but laugh. I mean a real belly laugh. How did they manage this? I didn't even notice them.

You look really pretty today
you look good in blue
it matches your eyes

I send a picture of the note to Gavin and wait for a response.

Atlas: Picture sent

Gavin: What the hell is that?

Atlas: I'm assuming it's from my stalker. You got any leads?

Gavin: I had a hunch, but after that note, I'm pretty sure your stalker is a woman.

Atlas: Did you find someone?

Gavin: I didn't see a face but there's a woman
in each camera feed around the same time
you mentioned feeling like you were being
watched. Similar characters each time– Long
wavy brown hair, same height maybe 5 '2 - 5'
4. Sound familiar?

There's no way he's saying what I think he's saying. So I do the only thing I can do, and ask him. I need him to confirm or deny it before I jump to conclusions. I thought I was seeing things. Could it really be her?

Altas: Are you saying it's Maizyn?

Gavin: Like I said, I didn't get a view of her
face. But it's possible it's her or Emily. What
do you want to do next?

Atlas: I need to catch her in the act. Do you
mind helping?

Gavin: You know I'm always down for a fun
game.

Emily

This is the first time all week I'm completely free to stalk Atlas as I please. With Trevor gone and me being off of work, I don't have anything better to do. This is actually the first Tuesday I've followed him, so I honestly have no idea where he's going. He left his office at nine-thirty in the morning today. Looking pretty good in a light blue dress shirt, might I add. Any other day, I've watched him, he doesn't leave until time for lunch. This is exciting! It's like an adventure. I note the date and time in my notes app and trail behind him.

We turn down third street and my heart beats just a little fast. This is the street we met on. Where we bumped into each other. This is the street that started everything. We're getting close to my favorite place in this town. Pages is right next to my job at the bakery. I was going to head there before my shift that day, but didn't have the chance because of him.

He slows his pace as he texts away on his phone. I match my pace to his for just a second before an idea forms. Opening my bag, I rip out a piece of paper from my notebook and scribble a quick note. While he's distracted by whoever he's currently texting, I get close enough to slip the note into his pocket before retreating back to a safe distance. It's risky but he didn't notice, so I think it was worth it. I can't wait to see his face when he finds it.

He enters the bookstore when he gets to it and my steps falter a little bit. I didn't think he would ever go to a place like this. Was this where he was leaving or headed to when we ran into each other? I wasn't paying attention that day. I didn't see him until after it was too late. I get close enough to the glass to peek inside and freeze in my tracks. He is sitting in my spot. That's MY SPOT– my chair, my pens, highlighters, my quiet corner, my SAFE SPACE– and he's sitting in it.

I take a deep breath and try to shove the chaos back down. I don't actually own the spot, he's allowed to sit there. It doesn't matter if that's my safe space, maybe it's a safe space for him as well. The panic starts to settle as I keep talking myself through it. Is it possible he needs that space just as much as I do? What does a man like him run from?

He reaches for his phone and I see the moment it registers that it wasn't the only item in his pocket. His brows furrow as he pulls it out and his eyes flash with interest the moment he understands that it's from a stalker. I probably shouldn't have drawn his attention to the fact that someone has been watching him, but I wanted to make it interesting. He unfolds the note and laughs. He fucking laughs, and it's mesmerizing. It's real, and I now know that I have to do everything in my power to make that man laugh again. I want to be the reason for it. He might not know it yet, but that laugh belonged to me. I think it's time I step up my game. Today's going to be fun.

He walks past the candle shop where I'm hidden at exactly twelve-forty-five PM. It's the same time every weekday morning. Always with something to eat that he gets from the Cuban place. I wait until he's far enough away before I make my move to follow after him. This is usually what I do when I have free time. I don't understand my fixation with Atlas, but I stopped trying to figure it out. I think I make a decent stalker. He hasn't found me yet, if that counts.

There were a few times I came close to revealing myself, but I always managed to save it at the last second. I follow him for a few minutes when he makes a left at the corner where he normally goes straight at this intersection. That's odd. I've been following him for weeks now and his routine is pretty solid, and pretty repetitive. Why is today different from the rest?

I speed past the few people in front of me to catch up. I don't want to lose his trail. I'm almost sprinting when I round the corner, but before I have even a second to look for where Atlas went, my head connects with the brick wall beside me. The impact isn't hard enough to do any real damage, but I'd be lying if I said I didn't currently see black spots in my vision. I try to shake my vision clear and attempt to look for what caused me to become one with this stupid wall, when a hand wraps around my throat, keeping me pinned to said wall.

Tingles shoot down my spine as I focus on how warm the hand around my neck feels. My eyes bounce around, trying to get the whole picture. It's definitely a man holding me here, and the moment my eyes stare into the light blue ones across from me, I know exactly who captured me. I felt my lips tip into a smirk. Those eyes could only belong to Atlas. Don't ask me why this man makes my body react this way, because I don't have an answer for you. Then it clicked, fuck, he caught me. How do I explain why I'm following him? What'll be the consequences?

Do I even care?

He shoves the left sleeve of my hoodie up to my elbow. His fingers tighten when he catches sight of the heart shaped birthmark near my elbow. "I fucking knew it," he seethed through clenched teeth. He chuckled, but it was laced with malice. "Oh Darling Chaos, what have you done this time?"

I met this man once and he's already giving me a nickname. I thought the stalking was crazy, but I guess I'm not the only delusional one between us. But why did that nickname give me goosebumps?

For a moment, it felt like my brain glitched.

Almost as if someone else's memory was trying to fight with my own. I tried to shake the fog away but it only increased the growing pressure in my head. I take a deep breath to calm myself slightly when I catch a familiar scent. Pine trees and mango. It was the same scent that always lingers in my spot in the bookstore. The same chair he was sitting in earlier today. This whole time, it was him. My obsession also happens to be the cause of the scent that makes me feel a little less alone in this world. The pressure continues to build as my mind struggles for answers. What the fuck is actually happening here?

Atlas

I slammed her up against the wall before she even saw me standing there. Thanks to my suspicion recently, and Gavin being my eyes, I knew I was being followed by a female that matched her description. This whole time I thought I was being stalked by a man. I probably would've figured it out sooner if I wasn't being biased. Imagine my shock to see that my stalker was Emily. Or should I say Maizyn? Now that I'm looking at her again, there's no doubt in my mind that she played me. I thought I was hallucinating this whole time, but that wasn't really the case.

If she has no idea who I am, then why the fuck has she been stalking me? She really thought she could play me? She should know I'm smarter than that. The fake name was clever, but pretending to be someone else was low. How could she run and let me think she was dead for months now? Fucking months! I was slowly losing my mind while she was reinventing her life. A life without me. Does she think that little of me?

I stare at her cataloging all of the tiny emotions flickering across her face. I freeze when I don't see the one I'm looking for.

She is scared, sure. I can feel how her heart is racing against the thumb I have pressed against her pulse point. Maybe she's a little excited if that smirk that touched her lips meant anything. But she's not scared that I caught her lying, no it's way worse than that. She's confused. I can see it in the furrow of her brows that something isn't adding up for her. She shakes her head like she's trying to block something out. My anger towards her starts to melt away.

How am I supposed to look at her when she holds my entire soul and blacked heart in her hands, yet no sign of recognition flashed in through those hazel eyes of hers? She looks at me like I'm a stranger. She looks lost in her own mind, and that fear I thought I saw, could've been because, to her, a stranger had his hand wrapped around her pretty little neck. While I want to hurt her for leaving me, she doesn't seem to remember that she even left me behind.

I'm not sure what hurts more, me thinking she was dead or her no longer knowing who I am while everything I have left shatters in front of her on this side walk.

I thought finding her stalking me was a sign she was lying, but not anymore. This has to be some kind of karma. I had to have fucked up bad enough to live in a world where the woman I should've married when I had the chance, doesn't even know who the fuck I am anymore.

I thought I knew what broken and empty felt like. I thought I hit rock bottom when she left and I thought she was gone, but this emotion I'm currently experiencing is a whole different animal. I don't think I'd wish this type of pain on my worst enemy. I shut my eyes tightly, trying to lock everything in. The last thing I needed to do was scare her more than she already seems to be. I'll get to the bottom of this fucking mess one way or another. Maizyn had to be in there somewhere. I just had to find her and bring her back. What happened after she left my house that night?

When I opened my eyes, I realized I still had my hand wrapped around her throat. I can't handle hearing whatever response she may have, so I don't give her the chance to say anything. Releasing her, I forced a smile that I didn't feel and began backing away.

Before I get out of ear shot I shout back over my shoulder "I guess I'll be seeing you around? Try not to get caught next time, it makes the game more fun that way."

I really hope I didn't fuck this up. I'll figure out what happened and I'll do everything in my power to get her to fall in love with me all over again. I just had to get her to take the bait.

Chapter Nine

Emily

Even though Atlas is aware I do a little light stalking every now and then, it's still pretty fun to keep up the ruse. It's become a game of sorts. He knows I'm probably following him and I try not to get caught. I've only been caught a few times so if you ask me, I'm winning. I know his schedule well enough, I can beat him to a location and hide before he even shows up. That's my plan today.

It's Tuesday, which means he should be heading to the book store this morning like he's been doing every Tuesday lately. Instead of walking to his office and following him all the way to Pages I decide on heading straight there. No point in wasting time if I don't have to. Plus the only way to get inside the bookstore without being seen is to get there first. I'm pretty sure he sticks to his schedule because he wants me to stalk him. I still can't wrap my head around his reaction to finding me.

He called me Darling Chaos like I belonged to him. The crazy thing is, for those few minutes with his fingers wrapped around my throat, it felt like I did. Something about that entire moment felt like déjà vu. Without having any memories of the last year, I don't even know if there's a reason for it. Why did I smirk even though he could've easily snapped my neck? Even with him angry and me pinned to the bricks, I felt safe.

My body's entire reaction to him was a contradiction. Being scared never crossed my mind, excited I was finally caught, turned on from being pinned to the wall, yes, but not afraid. I should've been at least worried for my own wellbeing, but I didn't care. All I could focus on, was the way this man looked at me, and that fucking nickname. The way it sounded when it rolled off his tongue. The words dripped with venom and love at the same time. My thighs clenched, and my heart raced at the simple phrase. It still echoes in my mind. I can't stop the endless loop from playing in my head. I felt my sanity slip a little more each day. Who was this man? And why did he feel like home?

Once again my thoughts keep me occupied until I reach my destination. I really hope I never make any enemies, I'd be too busy talking to myself to even notice someone before they killed me. It's like I completely black out. I can't tell you how I got here, just that my feet know where to go even when my mind checks out.

Entering Pages, I rush to my beanbag in the corner, knowing I don't have much time before he arrived, and I wanted to enjoy the moment. I sink into the seat and it engulfs me like a warm hug. The scent hits me immediately. That scent that belongs to my obsession and feels like home. All the questions about the events I can't remember swirl in my mind.

But all I have to do is close my eyes, and let this space shut the world out. His scent grounds me, the only sound I hear is the turning of book pages. All the unanswered questions don't matter. For just a few seconds, it's peaceful. I take one last soothing breath before opening my eyes again.

Unfortunately, I have a target to hide from and stalk so, I can't sit here much longer or he'll definitely find me this time. I slip behind the book shelves as I hear the door chime open. Perfect timing.

My eyes follow him as he makes his way inside. He does exactly what I expect him to do and plops down in the chair I just vacated. His lips twitch just a little, like he's fighting a smirk. He must sense me watching him. He always seems to know when I'm around, even if he doesn't always know exactly where I'm at. I would love to know what gives it away every time. I pretend to browse the shelves for a book.

You know, trying to act like a normal person.

I wouldn't want to draw too much attention to myself. A good stalker is supposed to be invisible right? Unmemorable? I see movement in my peripheral vision so I glance back in his direction but don't see him. How did he somehow manage to vanish in the short time I had my head turned?

I felt him before I saw him. His breath on the back of my neck was the first thing I noticed. I froze. The closest he's ever been to me was the first time he caught me, before we started this game we were playing. This was different. I felt the heat of his body through my clothes before he even touched me. He stepped closer, pinning my body between him and the shelf in front of me. One of his hands lands on the bookshelf next to my head. I can see he's holding himself back based on the way his knuckles whiten from his grip on the shelf. What's he stopping himself from doing, and what would it take to make him snap? I'm not sure if it's the smartest idea, but I want to watch this man unravel, and I want to be the reason for it.

My heart was beating out of my chest. I think he's close enough to hear how fast it was beating for him. His lips brush against my pulse point before he lets out a soft chuckle. Chills race down my neck and all the way down to my toes. My entire body breaks out in goosebumps. Fuck, he knows my body has a reaction to him. He can freaking see it. If only he knew how far my reaction really goes. He owns my body without even trying. His proximity alone has my knees weak, and my panties soaked. It's not fucking fair. His lips move closer to my ear.

"Who are you looking for, Chaos?"

The man was good, but he was as cocky as he was charming. It was infuriating. I both loved it, and it pissed me off.

"I don't know what you're talking about," I wasn't going to give in that easily. This was a game after all. I'm not going to just let him win.

"So you're not here for me?"

"Don't flatter yourself. I'm here to buy a book. This is a book store after all," His free hand grips my hip at my response. My skin feels like it's on fire, his touch burning. His grip on my hip tightens as he pulls me tighter against him.

"Ahh, I see my Darling Chaos is feisty today. Good to know,"

My brain malfunctions. He said his Darling Chaos like I was his to claim. If he wasn't holding me against him right now, I would be in a puddle at his feet. There's no way he meant to call me his. He didn't even know me, no matter how badly I wished he did. At my lack of response, he swings me around to face him, but I refuse to make eye contact. The last thing I need is for him to be able to see everything I was thinking written across my face. I don't even know why he's entertaining this.

Am I just a joke to him?

Not even in my dreams will I ever be enough for a man like him. He lets go of me and takes a step back. I expect him to leave, but I'm starting to learn he may never react in the way I expect him to.

Instead of leaving me standing there, he asks me a question. "What's your obsession with books? It seems too calm for you. You're always getting into trouble or doing something crazy. So why? What's it about books that piques your interest?"

No one has ever asked me that, so it catches me off guard when he does. I take a book from the shelf, taking a seat at a nearby table. I need armor for this conversation. I open the book and hide my face as I bare my soul to the only person who ever asked me to.

"Books don't judge me. It's okay to be invisible or to not be important enough to matter to anyone else, because books will always be there. It's okay to not be loved in the real world when I can escape to thousands of beautifully brutal love stories. Books quite the chaos. They're the only safe place to feel every emotion they inflict. So why not books? The books see me and let me be unapologetically myself. Why would I want to be anywhere else?"

I didn't glance up at him. I didn't want to see the judgement in his eyes, so I kept my face buried in the book. His silence made it pretty clear he was shocked by my response.

"Well, if you're going to stalk me, very badly might I add, the least you could do is let me take you out on a date."

Did I just hear him correctly? I peek over the top of the book looking to see if he's joking, but he looks serious. I play it off like my heart isn't beating out of my chest at the possibility that he may be interested in me the same way.

"Not interested." I didn't fucking want his pity, and I didn't need it either. I can survive without it. I'll be better off if we don't pretend that this could ever be more than what it currently is.

"Hmm. So you're not interested enough to go on a date with me, yet you've been stalking me for weeks?"

"What's your point Atlas?"

"Ah, someone has done a little research, because I don't remember ever telling you my name."

I duck back behind the book, trying to hide my reaction to this frustrating man. "Still doesn't mean I'm interested."

"It either means I intrigue you or you are plotting to kill me," He uses his index finger to pull the book away from my face, waiting until I make eye contact before he asks, "Which is it?"

I shoot him a cheeky smile, "you figured it out, I'm secretly plotting your demise. Took you long enough."

He simply raises an eyebrow at me, not even humoring me with a response to that. "Fine, I'll go on one date with you, but I'm not going to enjoy it." I pull a pen from my bag, then grab his arm and scribble my phone number on the inside of his wrist. "Text me, I might even answer." I don't stay for a response.

Atlas

This woman was as frustrating as she was persistent. I felt her eyes on me the moment I entered Pages. I always do. No one else in this entire world makes me feel the way she does. Now that I know she's my stalker, she's usually easy to spot. I don't always find her, but that's only because I don't try to. I let her think she's winning this game we're playing. I worry that if she thinks she's losing, she'll grow bored and move on.

I can't let that happen.

It took everything in me not to push her against the book shelves and kiss her. She still reacts to me the same way she used to. I thought the shelf was going to crack under my grip. I didn't want to push her too hard and scare her away before I even got her back.

I finally asked her about her book obsession and her answer floored me. I didn't think her answer would've been so meaningful. My heart broke for her. The fact people in her life had made her feel that way makes my blood boil. The fact I was one of those people makes me want to put my fist through a damn wall. My guilt eats at me a little more as the weight of what I did, how I treated her, really sinks in. I know I fucked up, but I didn't realize how badly until now. I don't deserve her, but I'm too selfish not to try to get her back.

I asked her to go out on a date with me. I thought she'd jump at the offer, but I should've known better. She made me work for it. She stalks me but still doesn't make it easy on me. She's going to be a handful and a pain in my ass, but she's worth everything she puts me through.

I want her back any way I can get her. Even if she never remembers me, I want her in my life. I'll do everything I can to earn her love again, but I hope Maizyn comes back to me in the process. I know her real name is Emily, but she'll always be Maizyn to me. There's a reason she told me that name, and I might not know what that reason was, but coming from her, I know it was a good one. She wouldn't do something like that for no reason. Maybe one day, if she ever remembers, she might tell me why. She'll always be my Chaos, no matter what name she goes by. I can't wait to see what tomorrow brings.

Chapter Ten

Emily

I stayed up late last night waiting for a text that never came. It's not like I expected him to text me, I figured he's just inflating his own ego to see if I'd actually agree, but that doesn't mean I didn't hope he would.

Hope was dangerous though, it left too much space to be disappointed.

I get dressed and drag myself into work. Sadly, I can't quit my job and become a full time stalker. It doesn't pay the bills. I wish it did, but I'm not dumb enough to think I'd make a good private investigator, so a job as a barista will have to do.

I get to work just in time to open the door for customers. I hope I don't look as tired as I feel. The good thing about working here is, I can get a blueberry muffin and a coffee while I work. It has its perks. I go through the routine of taking orders and making coffee. It's a pretty slow shift, so it's just me right now, Brooke will get here around two o'clock.

I don't mind working by myself. It keeps me moving, even on a slower shift. The multitasking keeps my mind off the text I never got. He still lingers in my mind, but it's not as heavy when my mind and body stay busy. I don't think there's anything that could make me not think about him completely.

The first few hours of my shift go by in a blur. It's already noon when I look at the time on my phone and see a text from an unknown number on my screen. My palms get sweaty and I grip the phone a little tighter so I don't drop it. This has to be a text from Atlas, right? It'd be too coincidental to be anyone else. I click on the notification and open the text thread. My heart pounds in my ears as I read the simple message on the screen.

Unknown: I believe you promised me a date.

What do I even say back to that? There's no way he was being serious. Before I have time to type back a reply, a throat clears in front of me. The older man looks mad that I have all my attention on my phone. Can't say I blame him though. I was so focused on my mini panic, I didn't even hear him come in. Shit, right, I was currently at work and should probably do my job instead of trying to figure out how to respond to Atlas. I could text him back later. "So sorry sir, what can I get for you today?"

"Just a black coffee and one of those apple turnovers."

I put a to-go cup under the spout, flipping the tap so it'll pour while I grab an apple turnover and bag it up. I hand the man the bag and turn back around just in time to turn off the coffee tap to stop the coffee from overflowing. I pop a lid on it and hand it over. "Here you go. That'll be $4.38 sir, and again so sorry for the wait." He hands me a five dollar bill and tells me to keep the change. *That's so kind of him to leave me a sixty cent tip.* I force a fake smile to stop me from rolling my eyes at this man.

At least we don't rely on tips here, and my hourly pay is decent. My phone vibrates a few times in my pocket, but before I'm able to check it, a line starts forming in front of the register. *That's just great.* I still had two hours before Brooke arrived, and I was going to get slaughtered by an early rush. I quickly pull my hair up into a messy bun and prepared myself for the clusterfuck that was about to happen.

I started taking three orders at a time. I'd ask them what they wanted while preparing the previous order. Luckily for me, most of the orders were for baked goods and that was a simple bag it and go. I rang up the order as I handed it to them so they could pay as I grabbed what the next person asked for. It may have looked like a chaotic mess, but to me, it was organized and that's all that mattered. I didn't stop moving. I thought I saw Atlas at one point, but I didn't have the time to check. The moment I stopped to take a break would be the moment I got behind.

Brooke came in just as the last few customers placed their orders. She didn't even have to ask how my shift went. She can tell that it was super busy based on the empty display case and lack of cleaning the lobby. I haven't been able to leave from behind the counter to clean, so it currently looked like a tornado hit it. She sprung into action immediately. She bussed the tables then started to bring out fresh desserts and pastries to restock up front. Once the last customer leaves, she takes over completely and lets me go home.

That was the busiest shift I've worked in a long time. I just want to go home. I want to put on some super comfortable clothes and eat brownies while I watch a movie I've seen a dozen times already. I'm exhausted mentally and physically at this point. My couch was calling my name. I put my headphones on and pull my phone out to turn on some music for my walk home, and notice I now have five unread messages from an unknown number.

Crap, I was so busy I never texted Atlas back. I didn't even remember he texted until now. He's probably so mad right now. Trevor always got rude when I didn't answer him right away. I start walking towards the house as I brace myself for the worst as I open the text thread.

> Unknown: It's Atlas by the way. I thought that was pretty clear from my first text but maybe you agreed to go on a date with more than one person.

> Unknown: Damn. I get left on read then ignored by none other than my stalker. That's just rude.

> Unknown: I'm serious about wanting that date though. What about tonight? Are you free?

> Unknown: I guess you really meant it when you said you might text back.

> Unknown: I went by your job and saw that you were super busy. I didn't want to bother you so just text me back when you're off work. Yeah?

So that *was* him in the bakery. I ignore him for hours and he doesn't get mad? Not what I was expecting. What does he get out of this anyways? I still can't figure out why he'd want to go on a date with me to begin with. I'm nothing special. Maybe he'll just stand me up. I've had it happen before. The cool guy asked me out on a date, I got all dressed up and he never showed. When I asked him about it the next day, he laughed in my face. Told me he was joking and I was stupid if I thought he would ever date someone like me. No point in refusing this date when I doubt he'll show up. I add his number to my contacts and text him back.

> Emily: So I'm busy at work and you go and decide to stalk me for once?

> Atlas: That's not really the point. So that date?

Emily: What about it?

Atlas: Are you available tonight for that date
you promised me?

Emily: Depends.

Atlas: Depends on what?

Emily: What your plans for the date are.

Atlas: I was thinking we could go to dinner at
around 6:30pm.

Emily: Sure.

Even though he most likely wouldn't show, I still wanted to know what he'd say. I put my phone back in my pocket and speed walk the rest of the way home. I smelled like stale coffee and sweat. I could really use a shower. Entering my apartment, I kick off my shoes, heading straight for the bathroom. As I wait for the water to reach boiling level, I strip off my clothes. I can't help but glance at myself in the mirror. I wouldn't say I was ugly, just average looking. I was far from looking like a model.

My stomach was soft and I had stretch marks. My walnut brown hair was long at the moment. It sits at the middle of my back until the next time I feel manic and chop it short again. I was usually fine with that. My thighs always jiggle a little when I walk. I always try to be confident in my own body though. No matter what anyone else thinks about the way I look, I know the right person will love my body, curves, and stretch marks included. Sometimes the doubt just creeps in for a moment. Something about Atlas is bringing up old fears.

Stepping into the shower, I let the heat of the water take over. I feel my muscles relaxing one by one as the water slips down my back, something about the hot water is always so relaxing to me. Closing my eyes, I put my head underneath the spray of water, letting everything sink in for a few moments. No matter what happens with Atlas, I couldn't let it get to me. I refuse to let my obsession with that man be my downfall.

The water starts to run cold and I quickly wash my body before shutting the water off. Wrapping a towel around myself and another in my hair, I walk into my room, putting on the first comfy thing I find. I wasn't about to get all glammed up for nothing. By the time I get dressed and plop onto the couch it's five o'clock. I guess I was in the shower a little longer than I thought. I order a pizza while I scroll through movies. Ten minutes later, my pizza is ordered and a random movie is playing. It doesn't matter, I'm not really watching it. Instead, I'm reading this new dark romance book I downloaded on my phone yesterday. I end up getting lost in the book. It's a reverse stalker, which is kind of funny given my actual life at the moment. It's the reason I downloaded it, if I'm being honest. The female main character in this book makes a way better stalker than me, but that's not surprising. I'm almost halfway through the book when my doorbell rings. That must be my pizza. I slip on my slippers and rush to open the door.

"Oh shit, you actually showed up," Atlas stood in the doorway dressed in a fitted black dress shirt and matching black dress slacks. He shouldn't be allowed to look this good. It really was unfair. My eyes drink him in before I remember to look at his face. Oops, oh well. He wears his normal smirk. Of course he caught me looking, it would be hard not to notice.

"Was I not supposed to? I thought you agreed to go on a date with me tonight."

I look down at the ground, avoiding eye contact. This is beyond embarrassing. My cheeks heat and I already know they're probably pink. I didn't think I'd have to explain to my obsession that I thought he wouldn't even show up to a date he asked me on. "Yeah, I did. I just figured you would stand me up."

"What gave you that idea?"

"It wouldn't be the first time it's happened to me, but it's not important."

He's quiet. I'm starting to worry he left me standing here by myself. I wouldn't blame him. I lift my head high enough to see him. He's angry. I can tell by the flutter of his jaw and the clenching of his fist. Great, the last thing I wanted to do was piss him off. The moment he catches me looking, it's like a mask slips in place. The anger is gone and in its place, sits a warm smile. What was that? Did I imagine his anger or did he hide it from me? He shifts, holding out a flower for me to take. I'm not really a flower person, but this one's different. This one seems to be made of paper, more specifically, it looks like a book page. My eyes tear up a little as I take it from him. This is probably the most thoughtful gift I've ever gotten and that's sad to say.

"If you don't want to go out with me, Chaos, you don't have to. I would never force you to do something you didn't want to do," There was that name again, only this time his voice sounded sullen when he said it. I knew he'd probably keep his word if I said no, but I felt he'd be disappointed if I did. I didn't want to disappoint him, but I also didn't want to give him the power to disappoint me either.

"Just forget I said anything, let me put this away and we can go."

He looks me up and down and smirks. "While I love what you have on right now and I think you look adorable in it, it doesn't exactly follow the dress code of where I'm taking you for dinner."

I glanced down to see what the hell he's talking about and my jaw hit the floor. How did I manage to forget I was only in an oversized t-shirt and fucking cow slippers?! This is the last thing I want this man to see me in, and we've had a full ass conversation with me wearing it. I'm mortified. "Really funny you ass. Were you waiting to make that joke the whole time?"

"I'd never joke about an outfit like that. If I had my way, you'd end the night in a similar outfit, except it'd be my shirt you had on."

Rolling my eyes, I step aside and motion for him to follow me inside. He chuckles but follows after me. I walk him into the living room where the movie is still playing, but I quickly turn it off. "Um, just give me like ten minutes and I'll be ready to go. Make yourself at home."

"Take all the time you need. I'm not going anywhere."

Something about the way he said it made me feel like what he said had deeper meaning. I didn't expect him to actually go on a date with me, and I know there's something I have to do first.

> Emily: I don't think this break will fix anything. It's probably best if we break up. This conversation would've been better to do in person, but I didn't want to keep leading you on.

I don't wait for his response. I don't think I want to deal with it right now. I know how Trevor can be, and I don't want him to ruin this for me.

I grab the first dress I see in my closet and throw it on. It's short and black, the right amount of classy and slutty. It shows the perfect amount of cleavage and hugs every curve, resting mid thigh. This dress is too tight for me to hide a knife under it, so I throw one in my small bag. My hair is still damp so I leave it down. I'm really hoping it doesn't get super frizzy, but I make sure I have a hair tie just in case. I put on a tiny bit of eye liner, but that's it, I don't really wear makeup so that had to be good enough.

All that was left was shoes. He'd be disappointed if he expected heels. I'd never be that kind of girl. Shit, he's lucky I even put on this dress. Skater skirts were the most girly thing I was comfortable in, but my main form of dressing nicely consisted of jeans or shorts with fishnets. Slipping on a pair of black converse, I head back into the living room where I left Atlas waiting.

I expect him to be sitting on the couch when I round the corner but instead, he's leaning against the wall. Soaking me in from the ground up, he chuckles at my footwear, but acts like he expected it. No snide remark and he didn't ask me to change? This may be a promising date after all.

The way his eyes drink me, as his eyes travel up my body makes my thighs clench tightly. I can feel the wetness start to soak into my panties. If he looks at me like that all night I'll be sitting in a puddle at dinner. This was going to be torture. He mumbles something under his breath about this being more revealing than the shirt I had on earlier, but I didn't catch the whole thing.

My nerves sky rocket as anxiety starts pumping through my veins. Why do I care so much about what he thinks? This is so stupid. I should've never agreed to this.

I turn my face away so he can't see the tears building in my eyes. "Is it too much? I'm sorry I can change. I didn't..." I stop speaking as his warm calloused fingers grip my chin. I feel his lips brush against my forehead. It's so gentle, I'm not sure if I imagined it or if he just pulled himself back. He lifts my chin until we are eye to eye.

"You're perfect just the way you are. I would never ask you to change. Now come on, let's go."

For some reason, his words make me break out in goosebumps. I can't wrap my head around what's happening. He said I was perfect, not that I looked perfect. He said he'd never ask me to change, did he mean my clothes? For the second time tonight, I feel like what he says means way more than just the words coming out of his mouth. I don't realize I haven't moved until I feel the shocking jolt of his fingers lacing with mine as he pulls me alongside him to the car.

The car ride there is quiet, but not uncomfortable. The radio is playing in the background and it's peaceful. I don't want to break the silence and mess something up, so I watch out the window as we make our way to the highway. I don't really care where we're going but, it's safe to assume we're driving twenty minutes to the next town over. Where we live is so small, you won't find anywhere fancy to dine at. Even though I'd probably be more comfortable in jeans at a local diner, this is a date and I would like to see what he planned. I know I have to break out of my comfort zone every once in a while, hence the dress.

It isn't long before we pull into the parking lot of an upscale Italian restaurant. It looks fancy, making me feel a little nervous. I've never been somewhere like this. Honestly, I can't even remember the last real date I've been on. Even with Trevor, it was only to the movies or we hung out at home. This may be more than I bargained for.

He meets me at my door before I can unbuckle, opening it for me, and stands in front of the door, holding out a hand to help me out. He turns his body in a way that has him blocking the view anyone would've had on me climbing out in my short dress. Maybe romance isn't dead after all. Who knew all it took was stalking a man you happened to literally run into one day.

We walk up to the host stand and the host greets us right away. After Atlas gives his name for the reservation, we're escorted to a table for two in the middle of the room. The lighting is low, but it's not dark. I'm honestly impressed and feel less nervous now than when I first got out of the car. *I can do this.*

Atlas pulls the chair out, gesturing me to sit. I place my phone on the edge of the table so it's out of the way, but not sitting in my lap. Unfortunately, this dress doesn't have pockets and my bag isn't big enough to fit the phone and knife at the same time. My phone vibrates with a text notification as the waiter greets us. I ignore it. Whatever it is, can wait.

The waiter presents a bottle of wine, but it's never really been my thing so I politely decline, ordering a margarita instead. I needed to relax a little but something tells me throwing back tequila shots wouldn't be appropriate for such a classy establishment. A margarita would have to do the trick.

The last thing I wanted to do was embarrass myself, or worse, Atlas. I could deal with embarrassing myself, but I really wanted this to go well. I slurp down the drink before the server is even done reciting today's specials. Atlas smirks but doesn't say anything. I haven't been listening to a single thing the waiter has said, so when he asks what we'd like to eat, I just point to a random thing on the menu without looking. I wasn't that picky, so I'm hoping I'll enjoy whatever I pick. Atlas orders a chicken alfredo then hands both of the menus back to the waiter as he goes to leave. I fidget in my seat. Not only is the silence between us awkward, but sitting in wet panties isn't that comfortable either.

He breaks the silence first, "You alright over there?"

"Yeah, I am doing just fine," I can't exactly tell him my problem, now can I?

"You sure? You seem nervous."

"I'veneverbeenonadatebefore." I mumble out like the sentence is one big word.

"Woah, slow down. What did you just say?"

"You're going to laugh if I tell you."

"Try me."

Fuck, I wish the ground would open up and swallow me whole. "Fine, I've never been on a date before. Are you happy now?"

"Happy that you told me? Yes. Happy I'm the first man to take you out on a real date? Also yes. But if you're asking me if I'm happy every other man before me refused to treat you like you deserve? Then the answer would be no. I'm pretty pissed because you deserve the world. But we can pretend this is just dinner if it helps."

To say my jaw hit the floor would be an understatement. Who the fuck was this man, and why did he make my heart beat out of my chest?

Our food comes out before I can even form a response. Good, I'm starving. I'm pretty excited to try whatever I ordered based on all of the dishes I've seen pass by our table. It all looks good. They place down Atlas's chicken alfredo first and it makes my mouth water. The moment they place my plate down, I know I fucked up.

I don't know what this is, but it doesn't look like something I'd enjoy. I'm not a person that'll send food back just because I ordered wrong so I grab my fork and prepare myself to eat whatever this is. I also don't want to seem ungrateful by not eating it. I bring the fork to my mouth, preparing to take a bite when I feel his fingers wrap around my wrist to stop me. He takes the fork from me and slides his entire dish in front of me, taking the one I ordered.

"Don't say anything Chaos, just eat the alfredo."

I nod my head and mumble a thank you. I don't know how he knew, but I'm so grateful. It feels like he somehow understands me. The first bite of alfredo is almost orgasmic. I can't help the tiny moan that slips out. He grumbles something that resembles "fucking hell" under his breath as he adjust himself in the seat, and grips his fork a little tighter. I laugh at his reaction, leaning slightly forward.

Dropping his fork with a clatter and clenching his fist, he glances to my cleavage then back to my lips before settling on my eyes. His eyes look absolutely feral. He looks hungry, sure. But he's looking at me like he wishes it was me spread across this table instead of his meal. He looks ready to snap, and for some reason, that makes me want to keep pushing his buttons. Knowing I can pull this kind of a reaction from a man like him makes me feel like a fucking goddess.

Game on then. I take another bite and this time I moan on purpose. I guess that's the tipping point because the next thing I know, he stands up abruptly and throws enough cash on the table to cover the bill, plus a generous tip. He grabs my arm and drags me after him . Such a shame, I really wanted to finish that food. That's what I get for pushing buttons.

He seems to be in a rush to get me home because he's throwing the car in drive before I even have the chance to buckle my seat belt. He peels away fast enough for the tires to squeal, and I already know without looking at the speedometer, he's speeding. I'm starting to think maybe I pushed too far. Did I piss him off? The tension is thick and continues to build, but I refuse to be the one to break it. I know a bomb when I see one.

We arrived back in front of my apartment pretty quickly, but I expected given the fact he did twenty over the speed limit the whole way here. He walks me to my door with his hand on my lower back. I fish around in my bag for the keys on the way there. As I unlock the door, I'm about to ask if he wants to come in, but before I can even open my mouth, he kisses the back of my head and walks back to his car. I don't hear his car pull away until after I lock the door behind me.

What the fuck just happened?

Atlas

Her fingers fiddle with the edge of the linen tablecloth.She fidgets in her seat, as if the posh restaurant itself is enough to make her nervous.Like being with me makes her nervous.

I want to grab her hand to calm her down, but I can't risk moving too fast.

I don't want to push her.

Her phone vibrates against the table. Normally I would respect her privacy, but when I see that it's a text from Trevor, I can't help myself. I quickly scan the text before she notices. *She broke up with him?* I knew he was in the picture, and I would've done whatever it took to win her back, but I'm glad he'll no longer be an issue.

The moment her margarita hits the table, she drinks it down like its liquid courage.

Would she relax more if I told her my heart already belongs to her?

When the waiter takes our order she blindly points to a random item on the menu.

She's probably too lost in thought to notice that she definitely won't eat it. I know her well enough to know she'll hate it, but will refuse to send the dish back. So, I order her favorite, chicken alfredo.

I finally break the silence and ask her why she seems so nervous.

It's a punch in the gut when she tells me this is her real first date. It wrecks me that not a single man has treated her the way she deserves to be treated, me included.

We were seeing each other for months, yet this is still the only time I've done this for her.

Add that to my ever-growing list of fuck ups and things I should make up for.

Our food comes to the table and the sour face she tries to conceal confirms what I already know.

I seamlessly swap our plates before she's able to get a bite of her dish. I refuse to let her eat something I know she doesn't like.

The moan that slips from her mouth around the fork almost unravels me completely. I've heard that moan so many times before, if only she remembered how many times I've made her do it. It takes everything in me not to bend her over the table and fuck her right here in front of everyone.

Instead of acting bashful at the sound, she does it again. *Such a fucking tease.*

She did that shit on purpose, and one day, I'll punish her for that.

I am trying hard as hell to be a gentleman.

I want to do it properly this time.

She's more than just sex, I don't want to give her the chance to think otherwise.

But then, her second intentional cocktease moan is too much at this point, pushing me to do something really bad to her I know, I'd regret later.

Instead of doing what my mind suggests, I throw money on the table and drag her out of the restaurant behind me.

The drive home is pure torture.

All I want to do is get my hands on her. That dress, if you could even call it that, hugs her body like it's painted on her. My dick twitches just from looking at her.

And that fucking little moan she let out at diner.... I was so hard I had to adjust myself under the table, hoping she didn't notice.

But of course she noticed and pushed it further.

The woman I knew always did.

Maizyn lived to push my buttons and it seems even as Emily, that hasn't changed.

I have to get her home before I cave. I'm not proud of it, but I can't be this close to her without unraveling everything. We get in the car and I drive her home, fast. Faster than I care to do, but I must. Before I break and take her. Before I throw all my restraint out of the window, we're at her apartment.

I walk her to her door, kiss the back of her head, and fucking run.

I run because I don't know what else to do.

I don't want to mess things up this time.

No matter how bad I want her, I can't let myself follow her inside.

Chapter Eleven

Emily

I haven't talked to Atlas in a week.

He keeps texting but I ignore every single one.

I can't even bring myself to open them.

I don't have the mentality for rejection.

That has to be the reason he ditched me the other night. Everything was perfect. The date felt like I was in a movie, and the chemistry between us was hot enough it could've sparked a match.

Yet, he practically ran away from me.

No "goodnight".

No "see you later".

No "I had a good time".

Nothing but a kiss to the back of my head followed by silence.

Plus, add in the fact Trevor's back in town. He's back to pretending like I haven't told him I wanted a break and needed time away from him. He's persistent and it's annoying the fuck out of me lately.

It's always what he wants and when he wants it.

It's like he's trying to control every aspect of my life.

Trevor left for work about an hour ago, and I feel like I can finally breathe again.

Having Trevor constantly hovering over my shoulder has been nothing short of suffocating. He's been trying to find out what I've been up to. I can't exactly tell him I went out on a date with the man I've been stalking, even if I did want to tell him.

So I lied.

I told him I've been at home reading, or at work.

One night with Atlas made me hate Trevor.

All it took was a single night of being treated like I mattered to realize, I deserve more than what Trevor will ever be willing to give me.

Maybe that was the point.

People tend to come into your life for a reason.

Atlas and I collided together like it was written in the cosmos.

No matter how fleeting it may be, I still crave this.

I still crave him.

It's about time I put on my big girl panties and talk to Atlas. If he's going to reject me, I want him to say it in person.

The problem with that is, I don't really know where he'd be at this hour if he isn't at home, and I don't really want to go to his house.

So I do the next best thing, I check Gavin's social media page. Thankfully that man posts every little thing that happens, and he posted a selfie with Atlas twenty minutes ago. Atlas's grin is tight, forced to probably make Gavin happy. It doesn't reach his eyes. Unlike Atlas's blue eyes, Gavin's honey colored eyes spark with laughter.

Seems like luck is on my side tonight because he tagged the bar they're at.

Looks like I'm going to a bar.

I will not be putting on another dress.

Nope.

I'm dressing for war.

I start off with my matching red lace bra and panty set. I'm planning to go out with a bang, if you know what I mean.

I pair that with a black skater skirt, thigh high white socks with garters, and a white crop top. I put my hair into a high pony tail and decided to wear my red hightop converse this time.

I slip my pocket knife into the garter on my thigh and take one last look in the mirror.

You can see my red bra through my thin shirt.

Did it look a little slutty? Maybe.

But Hell, I'd want to fuck me.

Let's just hope he will too.

This isn't something I'd normally do, but I'm going to fake confidence until I believe it. I can't let life just happen to me anymore. I'll never be happy that way.

Grabbing my phone, I take a deep breath and walk out the door.

You'd think a quiet walk to the bar would've been peaceful. Yeah, I thought so too. The only problem with that is, I was left alone with myself.

It would've been better to drive. The faster I get there the better. It's really hard to pretend to be this confident woman, when the voice in my head tells me otherwise.

I know I can do this.

I know this is probably just my doubt creeping in.

Do I still overthink everything and almost abort the mission? Possibly.

When I arrive, he's sitting at the bar next to Gavin with his back to me. He's dressed casually, all black. Jeans with a t-shirt and sneakers. There's also a black hoodie resting on the back of his chair. It's probably safe to assume he'd rather be at home than here.

But I can tell the moment he notices me because his shoulders go rigid and he stops talking mid sentence. He doesn't turn to look at me. If I wasn't watching his reaction, I wouldn't have noticed it. I don't think Gavin notices me, or Atlas' reaction, but he points to a blonde before laughing and walking away. He and the blonde somehow vanish as I make my way over to the bar top, taking his recently vacated seat.

I didn't get the chance to acknowledge him as the bartender greets me first. "What can I get for you, pretty little lady?" I swear Atlas growls next to me.

"Two shots of tequila, please."

The bartender winks at me as he pours two shots.

If Atlas doesn't leave with me, maybe the cute bartender will.

I reach into my bra to pull out enough cash to pay for the shots but Atlas stops me.

"Put them on my tab."

The rasp in his voice is a dead giveaway. He wants to say more but he's holding back. His knuckles whiten as his grip tightens on his beer glass. Is he mad I'm here?

Too bad for him.

I came to play.

I want to test my luck and push his fucking buttons.

I shoot a look at the bartender then flick my eyes to Atlas with the type of grin wild enough to burn shit down.

He reads the look on my face without any confusion but is he up for it?

Will he help me rile Atlas up just a little more?

He nods quickly, but it's subtle enough I almost miss it.

"Don't worry about it man. With a smile like that, her drinks are on the house," He smirks and walks off.

I throw back both shots without a wince.

Finally, I turn my attention to Atlas. He's livid and gorgeous. His eyes follow the bartender. He looks like he's seconds away from punching him, but I'm not sure why.

Wait a fucking minute.

I know that look.

Is he...?

Did the bartender make him jealous?

Well, poor baby.

The tequila gives me a confidence boost as I lean in to whisper in his ear, "Long time no see."

He takes in my appearance before responding. "I texted you. So many times. You haven't answered a single one, or even looked at them."

"You're not wrong."

"Was there a reason for it?"

"Nope. Just figured if it was important you would come tell me in person."

If he wants nothing to do with me then he can tell me to my face, not in a text. I also didn't want him to know he hurt my feelings by leaving so abruptly the other night. I wave over to the bartender asking for another round of shots. He pours them, places them in front of me and leans over the bar to whisper in my ear.

"Give him hell and if he doesn't work out or you change your mind, then you can always ask for my number."

I laugh and blow him a kiss as he pulls away to help someone at the other end of the bar. While his offer is tempting, I only did it to punish Atlas who's currently squeezing his beer glass so hard I'm surprised it hasn't shattered yet.

"Want to get out of here big man?"

"Why? You just got here?"

"Why not? What do you have to lose? We're just going for a walk."

The truth was, I was getting anxious and didn't know how much longer my confidence would last. I grab his hoodie from the back of his chair and toss it on his lap as I head for the door. Without looking behind me, I already know he's following after me.

Shit.

Now what?

I didn't think I'd make it this far.

Okay, I can do this.

I turn left at the intersection, glancing over my shoulder to see Atlas is still following me. Okay. Think. Think. We're walking right by a playground and a wicked idea comes to mind.

This grump needs to loosen up just a little, and I think I know a good way to make this worth his while. I grab his hand, pulling him towards the swings.

"You can't be serious right now. Why are you dragging me through a park in the middle of the night?"

I shoot him a devilish smirk over my shoulder but keep walking until we get to the swings.

Letting go of his hand, I gesture to the swing, but he just stares at me like I'm being childish.

Fine, we can do it the hard way.

I grab his shirt and pull him to me.

"Come on pretty boy, entertain me for a moment. I promise that you'll enjoy the outcome. What do you say?"

I know he's on edge.

I know he's still angry about what happened at the bar, but that's what he gets for just leaving the other night.

I push him backwards and he moves without a fight.

With a huff, he plops down on the swing anyways.

"I don't see how...."

Before he even gets the chance to finish his sentence, I use the ropes to pull myself up high enough to straddle him on the swing.

His hands automatically slip underneath the hem of my skirt, yet he still tries to protest, so I shush him by pressing my lips against his.

It's just a quick peck to stop him from over thinking this.

"Just swing Atlas.. live a little. What are you so afraid of?"

Instead of responding, his fingers trail up my thighs. They move higher and higher, until his left hand grazes over the knife I have strapped to my right one.

Eyes darting to mine, and he raises a brow.

"You think I'd go anywhere without one? I'm not stupid and this skirt doesn't exactly have pockets."

A small smirk twitches on his lips but he still remains silent.

Why is he not saying anything?

He lets go of me as his hands make their way to the ropes. He shifts our weight, spreading his thighs a little further so I sit flush against his lap before he finally begins to swing.

Sitting in this position, every time the swing moves forward or backwards, it causes friction where his jeans rub against my thin lace underwear. Rotating my hips adds to the tingling pressure that's already starting to build low in my stomach. I hear his sharp intake of breath as his grip on the swing tightens to the point his knuckles turn white. It's thrilling to get a reaction from him. Feeling his length harden against me causes a dose of adrenaline to buzz in my veins. Licking up the side of his neck until my lips ghost his ear I whisper, "How long can I tease you until you snap? Can I get you to fuck me right here?" He grunts in response so I keep going.

I knew I was already leaving a wet spot on his jeans. I could probably come from grinding against him just like this, but I wanted more. I wanted him. I undo his belt and reach for the button on his jeans, but he grabs my wrist to stop me.

"I bet you're soaked already. How about we up the stakes? If you can come just like this, without me touching you, I'll fuck you. How does that sound, Chaos? We both know that's what you want. So earn it."

My hips pause for just a second. I expected him to stop me, not encourage me to take it further. My center clenched at his words. This game sounded like it was going to be very enjoyable, at least for me. Who knows, maybe he *does* know how to have a little fun. Instead of continuing the small circles I was doing before, I started grinding my hips forward and backwards against him. Not sure how it's possible, but he grows harder beneath me. I shift a little closer to him in order to apply more pressure to the right areas when his belt buckle brushes against my clit. I let out a quiet moan and do the same movement again. Fuck, that feels good. I grind against him faster, the belt buckle hitting the perfect spot each time. His body tenses beneath me for a second. He's still swinging but I'm no longer sure if he's breathing. With the way his fist tightens further on the chains, it looks like it's taking everything in him to hold himself back from touching me. Good. I want him to feel as out of control as I do.

Atlas

I started spiraling the moment she climbed into my lap. No, that'd be a lie. I started losing it the moment she walked into the bar. I don't know how she found me, but my body was on fire the moment I felt her eyes on me. I haven't heard from her in a week. I haven't felt her watching me or seen her around either. It's been hell. I was starting to think she disappeared again, that's until she showed up tonight.

She used the bartender to taunt me.

I knew what she was doing, and I fell for it anyway. I'm out of my element though. What game's she playing this time? This is the Maizyn I remembered. The way she's acting right now is one of the reasons I started calling her Chaos to begin with.

It's in moments like this where she's unapologetically herself, she takes whatever she wants and will create a fucking tornado in her path. This is the woman I fell in love with without realizing it, until she was gone. I told myself we were playing this little game because it allowed me to be in control of the situation, but if I was honest with myself, I'm never in control of anything involving her.

She's always so stunning when she lets go. Any time she allows herself freedom from her thoughts, she glows. I can't believe I ever tried to extinguish that. I was so fucking stupid and I'll spend the rest of my life worshipping her like she deserves.

She may think she's the one coming unglued while she gets herself off in my lap, but the thin rope I have holding myself together is about to snap. Not touching her while she grinds against my dick and belt buckle is fucking torture. I can tell she's getting close. Her eyes are starting to glaze over, even at night, the green seems to spark with fire. Her thighs tense up and I stop breathing all together. I'm petrified if I breathe too deep or look away for a single second, she'll disappear.

I don't want to close my eyes and wake up in my bed to find out this was another vivid dream. I've suffered through so many of them, it's hard to believe something this perfect could be anything but a nightmare in disguise. Her movements are sloppy now. She doesn't care about anything but the release she's chasing and it's maddening. She shatters in my lap. Her eyelids flutter closed as she soaks me and I finally snap.

I don't want to risk dropping her so with my arm on the outside of the chain, I wrap her pony tail around my fist and yank her closer to me. She gasps as I crush my lips to hers and I breathe it in. I don't wait for permission. My tongue immediately starts fighting for control over hers. The kiss is messy and unhinged but it's still not enough.

Letting go of her hair, I grab her knife. With two quick flicks of my wrist I cut her panties from her body before putting the knife back in her sock garter. I quickly pocket the shredded panties with one hand as I snake my other hand between us. My fingers skim through her wet center. "Such a good fucking job. Go ahead and get your reward, baby girl."

She fumbles with the button on my jeans, quickly pulling me out of my boxers. She lines my dick up with her wet entrance at the same time she leans forward with a shit-eating grin on her lips. I have no clue what this woman is about to do, but I know whatever it is, it'll fucking destroy me. Her teeth latch onto my shoulder as she drops down, taking me all the way to the base in one single movement. Fuck, being inside her feels like coming home. She takes a few seconds to adjust to my size before starting to move.

"Hold on to the chains and don't let us fall, Chaos."

She listens without an ounce of hesitation. She was always submissive, at least with me, she just happened to be a brat about it. Submission was something you had to earn from her, and it was fucking stunning. I grab her hips hard to steady her and help guide her movements, probably hard enough to leave bruises. I hope it does, I want her to think of me every time she sees them. If someone would've asked me if I thought it was possible to have someone ride me while I swung on a swing, I would've said no, but this is proving me wrong. It's taking a lot of core strength on my part, but it's worth every second of it.

The way I swing, added to the figure eights she's doing with her hips, has my entire body on fire. I'm starting to get close. I can feel my release building in the base of my spine, but I need her to cum again before I do. I shift my hips slightly, lifting her before slamming her back down. She pulls her bottom lip between her teeth to try and muffle her moan, but it doesn't help much. Reaching between our bodies, I start making small circles on her clit. She's dripping down her twitching thighs at this point. I increase the pace of my thumb and guide her harder against me. She throws her head back in bliss, moaning loud enough anyone in a one block radius could probably hear her. Fuck it, let them. I grip her throat just tight enough to add a little pressure as we both cum together. I didn't mean to come inside her, but she didn't give me any other option.

The look on her face while she comes on my dick looks even better than I remembered. The moonlight glowing on her face makes her look ethereal. She looks so beautiful when she falls apart for me. Fuck, I missed her, but I can't tell her that. It's torture not being able to tell her exactly how I feel, but that's out of my control. I don't want to lose her by telling her she's already mine. I got to convince her to go on another date with me. I don't know who I am without her.

Chapter Twelve

Trevor

She's hiding something from me. She may think I'm stupid, but I know her well enough to notice when she's keeping secrets. She said she needed a break. Said she needed time to figure herself out. She's more delusional than I give her credit for if she really thinks I'll let her walk away again. We already had a break– when she decided to leave town in the middle of the night and change her name, thinking I wouldn't chase after her.

She had about six months before I came after her. I'll admit, it took time to find her under her new name. I had to hire a very expensive private investigator to do it for me. She had plenty of time for a break. I thought she left because she wanted time alone. She always complained I didn't listen to her, that she felt like she no longer knew who she was. I'm not sure what the fuck she meant by that, but I didn't really care either.

I figured when I found her she'd be lonely and ready to come back. She always seemed willing to do anything to keep my attention, so I didn't think this would be any different. I didn't expect to find her with a new man, but I was wrong. That was a hit to my ego. If she left me just to jump into bed with someone else, then that meant she thought I was the problem. I understand if she wanted time alone, but that didn't seem to be the case. No– she wanted to be away from me, and that just wouldn't do.

I was tempted to drag her back kicking and screaming, but fate had other plans. The slut may have opened her legs for him but, from what I can tell from following her into Lucky's a couple of months ago, she decided to run from him too. Seems she was making it a pattern, but that's okay.

I wasn't letting her get away again.

She could run and push me away all she wanted, but she belonged to me. I didn't put up with all her bullshit for nothing. I dealt with her for years and did everything I could to mold her into a woman good enough to be at my side. She owed me at this point.

I admit there were probably better ways to handle her running from me. Ramming into the taxi I watched her get into probably wasn't my brightest moment. It could've killed her, but my anger was in the driver seat at that moment. I'm not proud of it, but I saw her running again and blacked out. It's like I wasn't in control of my body anymore– anger was. I was driving one moment and when I blinked everything went black. When I opened my eyes again, her taxi was already flipping in the air. At the time, I probably wouldn't have cared if she was dead. My anger was a different beast. Angry me just wanted her back even if it was just to put her in the ground.

The taxi driver died the moment the car landed. It sucks he was an unfortunate casualty, but it wasn't my fault– It was hers. She put him in danger the moment she got into his car. She was in pretty bad shape when I pulled her from the car, but she was alive. Not sure what was better for her at the moment but she no longer had the choice to decide for herself. I did what any good boyfriend would do and I drove her to the hospital. I dumped her body in front of the emergency room long enough to ditch the wrecked car.

Thankfully I wasn't dumb enough to stalk someone in my personal car so it was easier to ditch the car at a random place without it coming back to me. After that, I came back to play my role of concerned boyfriend. I gave them her real information. The fake name she picked was fucking stupid anyways. Why would she pick "Maizyn"? It sounded like trailer park trash at best, and a stripper name at worst. I'll never let her go by that name.

I guess the wreck was worse than I thought.

They said the fact she was drunk could've been the only reason she lived. She was in a medically induced coma to help her heal. The doctor mentioned something about a brain bleed and a bunch of broken bones, but I wasn't really listening. It's not like it mattered to me at all. The doctor also mentioned due to the severe damage of the brain, there was a chance for memory loss.

Was it fucked up I was hoping it happened? Probably, but you have to admit, it would make the whole thing about causing a bad car wreck just to force her to come back, easier to deal with.

If she woke up with memory loss, I could play it to my favor. I could tell her whatever I wanted to make sure she was mine again. Imagine how happy I was when I got my wish.

I waited for her to wake up. Sat at her bedside like the loving boyfriend I pretended to be. I secured us both an apartment. I had a studio apartment for myself, but I made sure to get her a place with both of our names on the lease. I may've forged her signature to get it, but I was going to do everything in my power to make sure she couldn't push me away this time. She was in a coma for a few months. I wasn't complaining though. She's a hell of a lot easier to control when she's asleep in a hospital bed. I didn't have a plan yet for what to do if she did wake up with her memory, but luck seemed to be on my side.

When she opened her eyes, she had no memory of ever leaving me in the first place. It was perfect. I told her the bare minimum– she was in the hospital recovering from her leg surgery. I hid all her medical files, and due to the amnesia, the doctors agreed it was best not to tell her about the wreck. Something about the fact her brain could be protecting her from reliving the traumatic event and if I forced the information on her, she could go into a panic. I didn't plan on telling her anything in the first place so it helped that they agreed to cover up the medical files until I told them otherwise.

In her mind we were still together. I was the boyfriend she was in love with. Everything was going well and was back to normal. She was back to the way she was before she left. Well, she was the perfect girlfriend for a little bit, at least. She started insisting on space to recover. I wasn't going to give it to her though. I wouldn't push her but I wasn't going to leave her alone either. I didn't do all of this just for her to leave me.

She could ask for a break and all the space she wanted but with my name on the lease as well, there was nothing she could really do about it. I'll go to the apartment whenever I feel like it. I don't care that she broke up with me. I agreed to it because it didn't matter what she said, she'll always belong to me. She's delusional if she thinks otherwise. This'll blow over and she'll come to her senses. Her mind probably told her something was off. She couldn't remember and I definitely wouldn't be the one to tell her anything. I shut down her line of questioning every time she tried.

The entire time she was on the stupid crutches, I babied her. I brought her food and anything she could've ever needed. It was super annoying but I was nice enough to take care of her. As soon as she got off the crutches, she insisted on getting a job. I let her, not wanting her to feel trapped in the apartment with me. I granted her a small amount of freedom, I wasn't a complete asshole. She was allowed to work if she wanted to.

Looking back now, I feel like letting her work was a mistake on my part. She started acting differently towards me not long after she started. She no longer asked about her missing memories. I didn't have all the answers anyway, I only knew she left and I was the reason she no longer remembered. There was six months worth of time I couldn't answer for. She started shutting me out in any way she could. She'd spend her days off gone all day. I wasn't sure what she was doing and when she was home, she was always in her room on her computer. It started to feel like she was avoiding me. Every time I tried to make plans with her she was busy. I tried not to let it bother me, but it became impossible.

I even caught her staring at another man at the grocery store a couple weeks ago. It took a lot of self control not to ring her neck in the heat of the moment. I couldn't tell who she was looking at, but the fact it wasn't me made my blood boil. Don't even get me started on the fact when I grabbed her thigh in my truck on the ride to the store, she flinched. I knew it was involuntary but it pissed me off. She tried to play it off and act like it didn't happen thinking I wouldn't notice, but I did. She was going out more and I knew she wasn't at work, because I checked. I figured the best way to uncover what it was she was hiding would be to tell her I was going out of town.

I was fucking pissed when *he* showed up to pick her up for a date. How did he find her? Does she know who he is? I can't believe she's entertaining this man again.

For her sake she should be glad nothing happened between them that night.

They went to dinner and he dropped her back off. That was it. Maybe without her having her memory he doesn't want her anymore. She's pretty plain in comparison to what I think a man like him would go for anyways, and she was already mine, so she wasn't up for grabs.

I didn't give her much alone time after that. I couldn't let her think she could be with anyone else but me. I spent the week at her apartment even though she made it pretty clear she didn't want me around. I keep asking her what she's been doing lately, but she brushes it off and either says she's working, at the book store, or hanging out with a friend.

The problem with that story was, I already knew she had no friends. I gave her plenty of chances to tell me about him but she wouldn't, she was being cagey and would change the topic any time I asked. I guess that was fair after the way I treated her when she asked about her memory loss. I decided I wanted to give her space to see if she'd go to him again.

The moment I told her I'm working a night shift, she jumped at the chance to go see him, making it easy. I followed her to the bar and watched as she interacted with him. She's different around him, not acting like the Emily I've spent years building. With him, she's carefree and daring. I fucking hate it.

She convinces him to follow her out of the bar, assuming she was taking him back to the apartment, but I was wrong. They came to a stop next to the park before she dragged him towards the swing. What the fuck is she doing?

She pushes him down on the swing and kisses him. I'm too far away to hear anything they're saying, but that doesn't really matter. When she jumps up to straddle him in the swing is when I almost lose it. I want to walk up and rip her off his lap, but I need to see how far she goes. She starts moving in his lap and I look away. If I watch it, I know I'll lose control of my anger and snap. Is she really about to fuck him out in the open where anyone can see?

She's MINE but she's running around acting like a free bird. I stay rooted in my spot until I hear the unmistakable sound of her coming. If I don't leave now I'll kill her out of pure anger, and I didn't feel like dealing with the consequences of that. I needed time away to form a plan, but I have to do it without causing suspicion. I'll keep her whether she likes it or not. She didn't get to leave me after all the shit she'd put me through.

Chapter Thirteen

Emily

Atlas picks me up, placing me on the hood of his car. Not wasting a single second, his hands are on me immediately as he starts to peel my hoodie away from my body. I'm not sure what it is about this man that makes me want him no matter where we are. I don't care that we are in a public parking garage where anyone could see us– we could be on a crowded sidewalk and I probably wouldn't notice. When I was with him, the rest of the world didn't exist. I just want to feel loved by him. I don't care I'm only wearing a bra underneath, but he seems pleased to find that out. His hands tangle into my hair as he devours me in a kiss. His kisses always feel like desperation and devotion wrapped together, but I wasn't sure if I was alone in the feeling.

His hands leave my hair and start a path down my body. His fingers skim across the pulse point in my neck, squeezing lightly before he continues his path. Something about his fingers around my neck made me smile every time. His fingers trail across my collar bone like he's tracing them to memory. His hand skates around each breast, not actually touching, but enough to raise my heart rate. The man is good with his hands. His touch leaves a burning sensation in its path. My back arches off the hood, bringing my chest closer to him. He chuckles under his breath before giving me what I want. He kneads my breast through the bra, but his grip is hard enough it doesn't matter. He pinches both nipples before he continues on.

Once his hands reach my waist, his mouth follows the same path. My skin pebbles underneath the wet kisses and quick nips he's leaving as he makes his way down my body. I really hope the marks will last a few days. I want to be able to see them marking my skin when I need reassurance. I want the proof of his love on my body when I no longer love myself.

His tongue licks across the swell of each breast before biting hard enough to leave a bruise. I grab the back of his head, holding him to me– I want more. I don't want him to have the option of stopping. Using his teeth, he yanks the cups of my bra down far enough to release my nipples. They pebble as soon as they hit the air. He places a few wet kisses and nips along my ribs, his hands gripping tighter on my thighs. I wrap my legs around his waist and grind against him. He chuckles against me but continues his teasing, licking up between my breast and around each nipple, getting closer and closer with each pass, but still not touching them. Fuck that. I grab a fist full of his hair and yank his mouth down to my nipple.

"So impatient, Chaos."

Before I can respond, he flicks his tongue across my nipple before sucking it into his mouth. My back arches into him as a moan escapes my throat.

"Is that what you wanted?"

I just nod my head as he continues his assault, trailing kisses to the other breast before doing the same thing. He pulls my legs from around his waist and moves them to his shoulders as he drops to his knees between my legs. He bites my thighs as he gets closer and closer to my center. He blows against my core and my face heats with a blush. If I was as wet as I felt, then I was pretty sure he could see it.

"You're so wet for me Chaos that you soaked through these tiny shorts."

Biting me through the fabric, he pulls my shorts and panties to the side. He runs a finger through my folds, spreading my wetness around. He sucks his finger clean and moans at the taste before leaning back down and flicking his tongue across my clit.

Beep Beep Beep.

Beep Beep Beep.

Beep Beep Beep.

My eyes blink open with a groan. Damn it! You have to be fucking kidding me. That dream was so vivid it felt real. The wetness between my thighs told me it was real enough. I don't think I've ever had a sex dream before. I guess there's a first time for everything. I blink my eyes and I can still picture the entire dream. It feels almost like it's ingrained in my mind like a memory. I can still feel his hands and mouth on my body like he was actually there.

I reluctantly drag myself out of bed and get ready for my shift. I don't really want to go to work today but it gets me out of the house and away from Trevor. After all my time spent with Atlas, I get the sense of déjá vu more often than I'm comfortable with. The more it happens, the more I believe it has something to do with the events of the past year I can't remember.

I started trying to get answers from Trevor again, but still nothing. Trevor keeps brushing me off every time I ask about what happened. Every time I bring up the fact I don't remember something, or if I ask about my health records, he gaslights me and tries to act like I'm crazy. I know he's hiding something, I'm not sure why but I'll find out one way or another. I told him a while ago I needed time to recover from my surgery, that it was mentally taxing on me.

It seems to have the opposite effect I wanted. It's like the more I try to distance myself from him, the clinger he becomes. I always have to lie and say I'm working in order to get him to leave me alone long enough to hunt down Atlas and see what he's doing. Should I stop stalking Atlas? Maybe, but I don't think I can. Not until I figure out why my body acts so differently to him.

Why do I feel safer and more seen with a stranger when I can't stand being in the same room as the person I was supposed to be dating? I probably shouldn't have slept with Atlas until I figured out the Trevor situation, but it's not like we're still together. Despite how he tries to act, I've tried to break it off several times. He just doesn't seem to understand that.

He told me today he was going away for a week-long work trip, and he had to leave in three days. I was looking forward to him being gone. It means I might be able to go on a date with Atlas again. As much as Trevor seems like a good guy, I no longer feel for him the way I used to. I don't know what changed. I can't pinpoint the moment it switched either. I was with him for a long time, but it seems like my body knows something that I don't, which has happened a lot lately. I just wish I could remember what happened.

Speaking of Atlas, it's gone back to normal. Back to the way it was before our date. It's been a few days since I've talked to him. We didn't talk about the date or the swing set event. I was back to the shadows following him around like I didn't know what it felt like to have him touch me. It was maddening. I now know what it feels like to have him look at me the way only he does, but does that mean anything? Just because I feel the way I do, it doesn't mean that he feels the same. At the end of the day I'm still his stalker.

Will I ever be more? Do I want to be?

Chapter Fourteen

Emily

I can feel my mental health slipping.

Other than when I find the time to stalk Atlas, I haven't seen him. He hasn't seaked me out or made an effort to talk to me in person. I wasn't even being sneaky about following him, yet he acted like I wasn't there. Was he ignoring me?

I'm starting to think I messed everything up by sleeping with him the other night.

Was that all he wanted? Does he regret it? Does he regret me?

I can't believe I ever thought I could be good enough for someone like him. There's no way a man would want to be with the real me. Trevor spent years telling me that and trying to help me be lovable. I should've listened.

We've texted a few times but it's not deep. It's been basic small talk that leads to nothing. I can't exactly ask him to label what we are yet, but I thought what happened on the swings changed things.

I need to clear my head. I'd go to Pages, but it now holds memories of Atlas. Will I have to find a new safe place? The book store no longer feels like it belongs to me. Over the last few weeks, my spot started to smell like him. I think he owns it as much as I do at this point. That only leaves one other place in this town to go.

I climb up the fire escape with ease. I don't come here as often anymore, but it hasn't changed much. The first time I climbed up here, I was still walking in that stupid boot on my foot. It's a lot easier to climb without it. I get to the top and climb over onto the roof of the empty building. I think it used to be a movie store once upon a time, but it's been abandoned for a while now.

The view from up here is amazing.

The building is tall enough you can see almost the whole town from here. I climb up onto the raised ledge and plop down. It's probably not the safest decision to make, but my body moves before I even process it. My feet dangle over the ledge- swinging in the wind. It's kind of freeing. But the peace doesn't last long.

The voice in my head starts whispering almost immediately. It would only take me sliding another three inches forward to fall. I lean forward and realize I'm higher up than it looks. Three inches is all that's keeping me sitting on this roof top. My hands grip the ledge as I battle with the idea. It'd be so simple, but I wouldn't be the one living the consequences of this decision. I scoot an inch further and watch as my feet swing back and forth.

The people below have no idea I'm even up here. They're so busy with their own lives, they don't see the girl currently sitting two inches away from going over the edge.

Will anyone ever see me?

Taking a deep breath, I scoot back and climb back over the ledge. I run to the other side of the rooftop, making my way back down the fire escape before I change my mind. I don't think going up on that roof top had the calming effect I was hoping for. I could've jumped. It would've been so damn easy to do.

No one was there to stop me, but I didn't do it. I was two inches from falling off, but climbed back down instead. Even though the thought was tempting, I was still holding on to the hope I wouldn't always be my own worst enemy. I'm smart enough to know the voice in my head doesn't always have my best interest in mind. I've lived with my own destructive thoughts long enough to know that.

I have a feeling if anyone can save me from the chaos I battle, it'd be Atlas. If he sees me like I thought he did the other night, then he could be the answer to everything. But what if that was all in my head?

Atlas

I can't keep my mind off Emily and those fucking swings. She was breathtaking and she was every bit the woman I remembered. I know she was back to stalking me and I feel bad about keeping my distance from her, but I didn't trust myself around her right now.

I wanted to tell her everything.

She was still mine even though she didn't seem to remember that. Emily- or Maizyn- I didn't know the reason behind the name change or the secrets she seemed to have kept from me back then, but I'd figure it out. I needed answers before I snapped and ruined everything. I needed to know what caused the memory loss and I suspected it might have something to do with the limp she has every once in a while.

I started by digging up everything I already knew. Even though I knew her as Maizyn Lewis, she was also Emily Carter. The timeline adds up when I compare it to the intel that Gavin dug up on her when I first ran into her. There seems to be a gap in the information on Emily. It stops for a while, then picks back up around the same time Maizyn showed up and then disappeared from my life.

If she ever gets her memories back, I'll have to ask her the reason for the fake identity. I know she's not the type of person to do something that in depth without a reason. It was more than just a fake name she gave to a stranger in a bar. Her drivers license and everything matched that name. What was she running from? Or who?

I researched any accidents involving a taxi around the time Maizyn would've been in one, and the articles started popping up immediately. I guess the perks of a smaller town is that something like this is a big deal to the news reporters.

There seemed to have been no witnesses to the actual accident, but it states the driver died on impact. It mentions the taxi was hit from the side and went airborne where it flipped a few times. The reports state no one else was in the car when emergency response arrived, but there was other blood found at the scene that suggested otherwise.

I click on the next article and it's a grainy picture from a street camera across from the hospital showing a woman getting dumped in front of the ER. I could tell even from the bad photo it was her. The timing lined up and when the hospital was notified of the accident, they matched blood samples from her to the scene. They mentioned the woman had no form of identity on her when she was found but her boyfriend, Trevor Sinclair, arrived shortly after and identified her as Emily Carter.

Was she still with him the whole time she was with me? Did she call him too?

I keep digging for any information regarding her medical condition but the media doesn't seem to know much about it, just that she arrived in critical condition and got there just in time. I make a note to hack into the hospital files and keep digging for anything else I can find about the wreck.

After another twenty minutes of searching, it's pretty clear I already found out all the information I would find. I sent a quick text to Gavin. I can admit when I needed help and he was the fastest hacker I know. I could do this all by myself but I wasn't patient enough for all of that.

> Atlas: Hey man I need a favor. Are you busy?

> Gavin: For you? Never. What am I hacking this time brother?

> Atlas: How did you know I needed you to hack into something?

> Gavin: Haha, because it's the only thing that I am better at than you. Am I wrong?

> Atlas: Okay smart-ass you are not completely wrong. I need a medical file from the hospital database.

> Gavin: Shit. Okay what hospital?

> Atlas: Saint Lukas General Hospital.

> Gavin: Is it safe to assume this has something to do with Emily?

> Atlas: It has everything to do with her. I need answers and that's the hospital that treated her after the wreck. I need to know how bad the injuries were and what caused the memory loss.

> Gavin: Okay man. I got you, it shouldn't take me long.

I exit out of my text thread with Gavin and look back at the photo from in front of the hospital. If no one witnessed the wreck, who dropped her off at the hospital? Why didn't they stay with her or say anything to the press about it?

It's very possible the person who caused the accident is the same person that ditched her in front of the ER. I take a closer look at the image and spot a man climbing into a black car that has a lot of damage to the front of it. No fucking way. The same person responsible for the hit and run proceeds to drop one of the victims off at the hospital.

I feel like instead of answers, I only end up with more questions. I run the license plate through a software but it traces back to a rental company. I make a quick call to the car rental company but they're of little help. They reported that particular car stolen. I switch to another screen and search the tag for any police reports.

The results correlate what the rental company said. I was able to find a police report stating that the vehicle was reported stolen from Eazy Motors Rentals and was later found abandoned in a gas station parking lot days later with a lot of damage to it. The list of damage matches what little I can see in the surveillance footage from the hospital.

That little bit of information is starting to make the wreck seem intentional. But why would someone hit the taxi on purpose? Who was the target? If it was intentional then I don't think she was the target. It's also possible the driver was scared and panicked.

I decided to torture myself just a tiny bit more and replay the voicemail I got that night from Maizyn. Even though hearing the sadness in her voice wrecks me, I try to listen for anything I may have missed. Her sentence cuts off in the middle of her talking before the unmistakable sound of the taxi being hit follows.

I listen to it again and the picture becomes a little more clear. She was trying to call me when she was hit. I should've never let her leave that night. It's my fault she left. I should've told her about the tracker and explained to her why I put it there.

Wait a minute... the tracker, how could I forget about that? I was so wrapped up in finding her again I completely forgot the entire reason I put the tracker on her phone to begin with.

I didn't want to tell her at the time because I didn't want to worry her, but I had a good suspicion she was being watched. She received a few cryptic letters to the house that I destroyed before she found out. At the time, I was hoping it was someone pranking her, but I put the tracker on her phone just in case. I wanted to have that implemented so if the need ever arose, I would have access to her location. I didn't think she'd find it and I also didn't think she would've thrown her phone on the side of the road when she left me.

Hell, I honestly didn't think she would've left in the first place.

Would it have played out differently if I told her why I put the tracker there? If I could change the past, I probably wouldn't have put the tracker on her phone at all. It's not like it was any help to me finding her when I needed to anyways. Did she change her name to run from whoever it was that was watching her? I can't believe that someone in my profession missed all the signs.

I was so infatuated with her I let her close to me without doing any digging into her past. I should have. Maybe if I did, we wouldn't be where we were now. The beep of an incoming text pulls me out of my own head long enough to see the notification from Gavin. I have to give credit where credit is due, the man works fast. It's an honor to call him my best friend.

Gavin: Are you sure you want to know?

Atlas: I need answers Gavin.

That made my stomach sink to my feet. If he was telling me this before I even saw the files, then it must be bad. Gavin has never warned me like this before. I download the zip file and start undoing the encryption right away. Each second feels like an hour as I watch the loading bar go from zero percent to one hundred. The images on my screen are like a punch to the gut.

She looks so broken and tiny in that hospital bed. Her eye is swollen with several deep purple bruises on her face, her leg is in a cast, and her arm is in a splint. I swallowed the bile rising in my throat knowing I could've stopped all of this from happening. I dig deeper into the medical files. They mention her blood alcohol level could've been the only reason she survived the crash.

Each file I click through only makes it worse.

Several x-rays, each showing a different broken bone. Fractured ribs and arm, a hair line fracture in her orbital bone. It seems like her leg got the worse of it. Her ankle had to be reconstructed with surgery, as well as a broken fibula. The next image I see is a copy of her CT scan. It shows slight swelling and a brain bleed. My poor girl, she didn't deserve to go through all this trauma.

I keep flipping through more medical files. There are pages mentioning the doctors deciding to put her in a medically induced coma until they got the bleeding and swelling under control. The more I read, the more my guilt built. I pushed her away and caused this. She doesn't remember me because I wasn't man enough to love her like she needed me to.

I read every single page Gavin sent over. I stop when I come to a page mentioning possible amnesia. From what I read, she woke up from the coma not remembering the wreck or anything related to arriving at the hospital. The doctor notes that they thought it was best not to tell her all the details in case the memory loss was her body's way of protecting her from reliving it. The doctor also stated based on his evaluation compared to the MRI and CAT scans, it doesn't seem like there's any physical reason for her not to remember and that the patient mentioned missing six months to a year's worth of memories. That the memories could come back on their own or not at all. It also stated that telling her what happened could trigger a panic attack or psychotic break.

FUCK! FUCK! FUCK!

What the hell am I supposed to do? I don't want to make this worse for her. That doesn't leave me much choice. I can't live without her so I'll earn her back the hard way.

Chapter Fifteen

Emily

Trevor left this morning so I can finally stop worrying about trying to ditch him. I still haven't talked to Atlas, so when my text notification goes off, I expect it to be Brooke from work or Trevor complaining about something. When I see Atlas' name on my phone, I freeze. Is this where he tells me to leave him alone? I take a deep breath and open the text thread anyways.

Atlas: What do I have to say to convince you to go out with me again?

He doesn't talk to me for days and this is the first thing he says to me? What is his angle?

Emily: Nothing. I'm not interested.

Atlas: Anything you want, I'll make it happen.

Emily: You would have to chase me in the woods and catch me first.

Atlas: Done.

Emily: What? I was joking. I didn't think you'd agree to it. I literally said the first thing I thought you would say no to.

Atlas: Don't try to play it off. I know you enough to know you wouldn't have said it if some part of you didn't mean it. When's your next day off?

Emily: I'm off tonight and then again on Friday.

Atlas: Friday is four days away. I don't want to wait that long. I'll pick you up at 9pm. And Chaos, I will show up for our date, on time. If you're not ready when I show up, I'm taking you anyway, no matter what you do or don't have on. Dress however you like. I'll even give you my T-shirt if you want it. The less you wear the easier you make it for me.

Emily: Whatever.

Atlas: Stop rolling your damn eyes and be ready by 9.

Emily: How did you know I was rolling my eyes?

Atlas: Because I know you.

I left him on read. He may have guessed correctly, but I wasn't about to tell him that. I guess he wasn't giving me a choice on him picking me up, and I trusted him enough to believe he'd keep his word. Leave it to him to joke about the freaking shirt I was wearing when I answered the door for our first date. He wanted easy access? Fine I'd give him easy access, and make him fucking drool in the process. I had three hours to get ready and I wanted to make this man miserable.

I take a long, hot shower, making sure to shave everything and exfoliate my skin. I wanted his hands on me, and I didn't want him to let go once they were. The self doubt tried to drag me back down but I threw that bitch in the closet and locked the fucking door. I just wanted one day to feel confident enough that I didn't try to ruin everything. I exit the shower and blow dry my hair. I leave it down, the natural waves reach a little further than the center of my back. Exiting the bathroom I dig in my dresser looking for the perfect thing when my hands close around a matching red lace bra and panties set. Just what I was looking for.

I pair the matching set with red fishnets and my red converse. Tucking my knife into my red thong, I clip it into place. I put on a light layer of makeup, nothing special– eyeliner, mascara, and lipstick. Then I wait for him on the couch. If he wanted to joke about giving me his t-shirt I'd answer the door in nothing but fishnets and lingerie and take him up on that offer.

There's a knock at the door and I practically prance to answer it. After checking to make sure it's Atlas, I throw the door open and walk back towards the living room. Looking back over my shoulder I catch him staring at my ass, but he hasn't moved from his spot.

"Do you plan on coming inside or are you going to stand there all night?"

"Shit, uh yeah my bad."

His eyes never leave me as he walks in and slams the door behind him. "Is that all you're wearing? Pretty sure I said I was going to take you even if you were not ready."

"Yeah. I know what you said. I also remember you mentioning I could wear your shirt if I wanted to. Or was that a lie?"

I hold one hand out to him for the shirt and my other hand is propped on my hip. He looks stunned. He glances from my eyes to my hand, from my hand to my cleavage, back to my hand before it seems like what I just said finally clicks into place. I swear he mumbles something under his breath that sounds a lot like "she's trying to kill me" but I'm not a hundred percent sure.

He pulls the shirt from over his head in one fluid motion and I can help but trace the line of hair that leads to the waistband of his jeans with my eyes. It's not my fault the man looks edible, you can't blame me for looking. I take the shirt from him and throw it on. I purposefully bend over in front of him to grab my phone before walking back out the door. He follows without a single word and we climb into his car.

Not really sure why I thought my lazy ass could run through the woods. I thought it'd be fun. It's something I've always wanted to do. I've read about it plenty of times. It seemed easy enough on paper. All I wanted to do was get chased through the woods by a masked man and get railed when I got caught. Seems like a simple request right? What the actual FUCK was I thinking?! I took two damn steps and already face planted in the fucking mud.

TWO STEPS!

That's it, that's as far as I got before embarrassing myself, and of course he saw me eat shit and he laughed. He fucking LAUGHED!

I picked myself up off the ground and tried to scrape my pride off the mud and leaves, but it was hopeless. I was utterly embarrassed! So much for recreating a spicy book scene. I huffed out a breath and was turning back to leave when he grabbed me by my throat and pulled me to him. I refused to look him in the eye. I know he's going to mock me and say this was a dumb idea to begin with. I don't know why I even asked him to do this with me. I'm so dumb.

I should've never even mentioned this to Atlas.

I never thought he'd agree so easily when he asked what it'd take for another date. I was honestly joking thinking he'd say no. I would've been better off ignoring that text completely, saving me the trouble of looking stupid in front of him.

His other hand trails up my back and tangles into my hair. With a sharp tug, he pulls my head back until I have no choice but to make eye contact.

I wasn't expecting the emotion that reflected in his icy blue eyes. Instead of amusement, I was greeted with heat and lust. His arrogant smirk was still present, but his eyes were heavy-lidded and were a shade darker than normal.

"You know I love when you get all dirty for me my Darling Chaos, but mud wasn't exactly the substance I thought I'd see you covered in."

I rolled my eyes and tried to pull away from him, "this was stupid, let's just go. It's not like you wanted to do this with me anyways." He makes a sound that resembles a growl and flexes his fingers a little tighter around my neck.

Bringing his lips to my ear he whispers, "Okay my bratty Little Chaos, you know I love you a lot right?"

There's no way I just heard him correctly. Did he just say LOVE? How could he love me when he barely even knows me? Nope there's no way he said that. I was speechless. I nod my head instead of trying to string together words. The way his fingers feel wrapped around my neck makes my pulse race and my thighs clench. This doesn't feel real. I wait for him to correct himself, but he doesn't.

"Good", he grunts. "I'm going to need you to remember that because this attitude of yours needs to be fucked out of you. When I catch you, I'm going to fuck you like I hate you, do you understand?"

My eyes glaze over and heat travels through my body as I nodded again.

"Tsk, tsk, tsk, you know that won't work for me baby girl, use your big girl words. Do you understand?"

I know exactly what he wants to hear so I don't think about it, "yes si...yes, I understand." Shit that was not what was supposed to come out of my mouth, it just slipped.

His lips tip up into a smirk, his eyes darken just a little more as his fingers flex a little tighter around my neck. "No, that won't do. Say what you were going to say. I bet you won't."

If he wants to play games, fine we can play games. I rolled my eyes again and took a tiny step closer to him. I already know I'm going to enjoy every deprived thing he's about to do to me. "Yes, Sir. I understand. Are you happy now?"

He lets go of me like I burned him, dropping his hands to his side before reaching into his back pocket and pulling out a ghost face mask. He gives me one last smirk before he pulls his mask down over his face. "Now Chaos, fucking run."

I take off sprinting into the woods again while his muffled laughter rings around me. I didn't take him as the type to enjoy this, but damn am I glad I was wrong.

Atlas

She may not remember, but her body does. Somewhere in there she's still Maze. To her this is the first time she has done this with someone she's just getting to know. To me, we've done this several times and I'm hoping it'll jog a memory. I really enjoy how she reacts to the chase.

I slipped when I said I love her. Not because I don't, but because I do and I know she's not ready to hear that. Lucky for me she didn't even react to it. She just had to test me by being a fucking brat. She was always pushing my buttons. It's like she enjoyed making me snap, and it seems that hasn't changed a bit. The little fucking tease show she pulled on me when I picked her up only pushed me further over the edge. If I wasn't trying so hard to control myself, I would've bent her over her couch and fucked her there. It's so damn frustrating that I'm stuck remembering everything, and she's clueless.

Setting the timer on my phone, I give her a five minute head start. She's clumsy as hell so she'll definitely need it. I don't want to rush this even though my painfully hard dick is begging me to. I know it'll be much more enjoyable the longer I drag this out. It's been months since I've been able to get my hands on her the way I truly want to. I'm not going to waste this time by rushing it. Yeah, she may have fucked me on the swing set, but that's tame compared to what I'm about to do.

My timer finally signals the end of the five minutes. I slowly trail after her but I don't mask my footsteps. I want her to hear me coming. It's the anticipation that gets her every time. I hear a thud to my right and her muttered curse.

She must've tripped again.

I swear she has two left feet. I peek around a tree without giving myself away and I'm not at all surprised by what I see. She's picking herself back up off the ground and brushes her dirty hands off on my shirt that she's wearing. She looks so pretty like that, in my shirt, covered in mud and waiting for me to pounce. She's adorable and maddening at the same time. She has sticks and leaves stuck in her hair and I can't help the laugh that bubbles up in my throat. Her head snaps in my direction and she freezes in place. Oops... I guess I gave myself away.

Emily

Even though I know it's him behind the mask it's like my feet are frozen in place and my heart rate increases. Excitement mixed with a small amount of fear. The moment he takes a step towards me, I'm off like a startled animal. My heart is pumping so loud I can hear it above my heavy breathing, over the sound of the crunching leaves and snapping sticks behind me. This feels primal and thrilling. Even though I'm scared I can feel my arousal build between my legs. The closer his footsteps get, the wetter I am. It's so freeing.

I feel his fingers snag my hair and it's like time slows down, all the color dulls for a few seconds. It almost feels like I'm seeing the scene play out in my head.

Using my hair as a tether, he yanks me close enough to him so his arm can snake around my waist. The moment he has me in his grasp, he throws our weight forward sending us barreling to the ground.

As soon as my hands are embedded into the mud, time speeds back up to normal speed and the color blooms back, even more vivid than before. Something about this feels so familiar, but I can't put my finger on it. What kind of fucking mind games was my brain trying to play on me now? I'm not a ghost, I'm real and I'm here with Atlas, at this moment. I repeat it a few more times in my head. My attention snapped back to the world around me when Atlas' hand in my hair pushed my head down into the mud. I'm not sure why, but even this felt safe with him.

Does that mean I'm broken?

Atlas

My fingers tangle into her hair and I yank her into me. As soon as I get my hands on her, something snaps. It doesn't matter how hard I fucking tried to keep some semblance of control, it crumbled the moment she ran. It's like I'm no longer in control of my body and I'm acting on instinct alone. She's MINE and I'm about to show her who she really belongs to. Her body is mine to play with however I please, even if her mind doesn't remember that right now. Nothing about what I was about to do to her would be soft. I'm going to fuck her like I hate her, I just hope she's ready for it. I shove her face into the mud below us and wait a few moments to gauge her reaction. She doesn't scream, but she's still trying to wiggle free.

"Safe word?"

"What?"

"Pick a safe word. I'll not stop until you say the safe word, so fucking pick one."

"SPOON!"

"Spoon?"

"That's what I fucking said isn't it?"

"I don't think you're in the position to have an attitude, Chaos."

"Fuck you."

"Oh I will in just a moment don't you worry your pretty little head about that. Spoon it is. Don't forget your safe word, brat."

I keep one hand on the back of her head, holding her still while I run my other hand up the outside of her right thigh until it lands on what I'm looking for. I know she always carries a knife on her and I plan to use it to my advantage. I raise the shirt over her ass so I can see how it's clipped in. She normally goes for some kind of holster, and I was so busy staring at her ass earlier that I didn't get a good look at it.

Fuck me, my dick grows harder against my zipper when I find her knife clipped onto her fucking thong.

I can't explain it, but knowing she could stab me if she damn well wanted to, causes all of my blood rushing to my dick. I adjust myself before leaning down to press a kiss to her lower back. Trailing the kisses to her hip, I bite down as I pull the knife free. She falters and I get to work cutting away the fishnets and her panties. I have an extra shirt in the car, so even though I like how she looks in my shirt, I start to cut that away from her body too. It takes both hands to cut through the shirt. The moment my hand leaves the back of her head she kicks out at me connecting with my chest and tries to run again.

She doesn't get far. My hand wraps around her ankle and I drag her back to me, straddling her thighs so she can't escape this time. I use the discarded fishnets to tie her wrist behind her back.

"Let go of me, asshole."

"No can do, sweet cheeks. You know how to make this stop and that's not it."

She continues to kick and buck beneath me as I continue to cut the shirt from her body and I'm loving every second of it. Based on the wetness dripping down her legs, she does too. I slide back a little further so I'm sitting on her calves instead, pulling her hips up until her ass is in the air for me.

"Such a pretty mess for me, Chaos." I smack her left ass check before soothing it with my hand and repeating the same thing on the right. She looks so good with my hand prints on her.

She's no longer fighting below me. Her body almost seems to melt under my touch. It's always so beautiful when her body submits to me. Even if her mind tells her I'm a stranger, her body still trusts me. I lick up each thigh before sinking my teeth into her already red ass check. She moans loud for me as I spread her lips and my tongue swirls around her clit. I continue the circles getting closer and closer to that bundle of nerves. As soon as my tongue flicks against it, I suck her clit into my mouth and bite. I continue working her as I insert a finger inside of her. My control isn't going to last much longer but my girl will always come first. I add another finger and curl them so I'm hitting her G spot with each thrust. Her legs begin to quiver as she tightens around me. I know she's getting close. I speed up my movements. She comes apart on my fingers and I don't stop until her climax is over. I remove my fingers from her and lick up all of the mess she made. Fucking delicious.

I pull her upper body up by the back of her neck, turning her around, and use her knife again to cut her bra from her body. I bite and suck each nipple until it's rock hard for me before standing to my feet. Her pupils are so dilated they're almost black, and I fucking love it. I undo my jeans and lower them just enough to pull my dick out.

"Open."

She doesn't even hesitate before opening her mouth and sticking out her tongue. I slap the head of my dick against her tongue before shoving it down her throat. She gags around me and her eyes flare with anger, but she stays quiet.

"You poor baby. Is my brat not getting her way?"

I shove it back in until I'm sitting in the back of her throat. "Where did that attitude go? Nothing to say now?" If looks could kill, I'd already be dead. But I can't help but bait her when I know she can't respond. She tries to say something around me but I push forward until I cut off her air supply. "Behave and I'll give you what you want." She nods her head and I pull out to let her breath.

"You're going to let me fuck this pretty mouth until I cum, and then I'll fuck your pussy like you want me too. Does that sound good?"

"Yes."

"Yes what?"

"Yes, sir."

"Good girl."

I thrust back into her mouth over and over again. My fingers wrap around her throat and I can feel it every time she swallows me. She gags a few times and her eyes are watering, but I can tell by the look in her eyes that she's enjoying every second of it. I'm already close when she swallows around me again. I pull out just in time to cover her face in my cum.

"Now you're covered in something better than mud."

She collapses back down into the mud trying to catch her breath as I move back behind her. Even though I just finished, I'm already hard and ready to go again. This woman drives me wild. I don't think I can ever get enough of her.

I push her knees wide enough apart that I can fit between them. I rub my dick through her wet folds before pushing all the way inside of her in a single thrust. She flutters around me as I pull out and snap my hips against her again.

Reaching between our bodies, I rub her clit as I continue to thrust in and out of her. After several more thrusts, she shatters against me, screaming my name in the process, and I climax right after her. This fucking woman is mine and I'll do everything in my power to win her back. I fully empty myself inside of her like I have every right to. After I've caught my breath I slip my dick back into my jeans, pocket her knife and scoop her into my arms.

"Let me take you home, Darling Chaos." She doesn't say anything, just nuzzles into my chest as I walk her all the way back to the car.

Chapter Sixteen

Atlas

By the time I get her back to my car she's fast asleep. Even though the walk was a little further than I thought, and her hair tickled my face the entire walk back, I'm not complaining. I'm soaking up every blissful moment of carrying her. I squeeze a little tighter, keeping her pressed to my chest. I hold her to my body with one hand while I use the other to open the passenger car door. I hesitate, not wanting to put her down. Here, while she's wrapped in my arms, she's mine again. I can pretend, even if only for a few seconds, that she knows how much she means to me. For just one quiet moment, I can pretend she didn't forget every single thing about me- about us.

I'm scared that if I break this moment, I'll never have it again— more than scared— I'm completely petrified. I don't want her to only be mine in stolen moments like this. It's pure fucking torture. The messed up part about the whole thing is I know I deserve this. I took her for granted and the world took her from me. I'm not stupid, I know I messed up. I know I should've treated her better when I had the chance, but I don't think I'll survive in a world without her next to me in it.

I lean down and gently place her into the passenger seat trying my best not to wake her. While I don't mind the view, I can't exactly leave her passed out, covered in mud and naked in my passenger seat, so I quickly grab the extra shirt I had in the back seat just in case of this moment. I put the shirt over her head, pulling it down her body. She jostles just a little bit as I struggle to get her arms into the correct holes.

A soft murmur passes her lips but she doesn't wake up. It was so quiet, I couldn't even hear what she said. I feel kind of guilty that she's so tired. It wasn't my attention to be so rough with her, but her and that bratty attitude she wields always makes me snap. The ache in my chest tightens a bit more as I fasten the seatbelt around her body. Even after everything, her body still feels safe enough to be this vulnerable around me. I press a soft kiss to her head.

"I'll always love you, Chaos."

The words tumbled from my lips before I could even try to stop them. I freeze. I don't move an inch while I wait to see if she hears me. After a few seconds without a reaction, I exhale a breath I didn't realize I was holding. Thankfully, she's still sound asleep. I don't think that is a conversation I'd be able to have with her right now. I know she's not prepared to hear it. If she's ever ready to hear these words from me again, I'll tell her every single chance I get.

It takes everything in me to pull myself away from her, but I know that I have to. I step back from her and close the door behind me. Rounding the front of the car as fast as possible, I slip into the driver seat, shutting the door as quietly as I can. Not being close enough to hold her feels like we're worlds apart.

Cranking up the car, I reverse back onto the side road and start heading back to town. I don't realize how rough the roads are until I swerve a few times, avoiding any pot holes so she'll sleep fine. I don't want to wake her. She shifts slightly in the seat when I swerve a little too sharp.

My t-shirt rides up, revealing more of her creamy thighs. My eyes linger on where the hem of my shirt sits for just a few seconds longer before I reluctantly tear them off her and aim them back towards the road. I take a deep, grounding breath, white knuckling the wheel hard enough to strangle it if it was able to breath in the first place. My hands ache, but I'm trying to do everything to keep my hands off her.

The original plan was to take her back to her apartment after this and we'd go out on the actual date part another time. I know the right thing to do. I know what I should do, but I don't know if I can. I need more time with her. I'm not ready to leave her yet.

I debate my choices the rest of the way back to town. I make a mental pros and cons list, but it's no help. The ache in my chest increases just a little more. I know the moment we make it back into town and I turn left heading towards my house instead of making the right to her apartment that I'm probably being selfish. I hope I'm not pushing her too far but I'm grasping for fucking straws at this point.

I tell myself maybe her spending time with me at my house will be a good thing. Maybe it'll jog her memory even just a little. I try to convince myself that maybe spending time with me in my space will make some kind of difference. It honestly doesn't matter what lie I try to tell myself while glancing over to her as she sleeps peacefully in my car, I feel it. Fear, loss, regret– the list goes on. But one thing is really clear. I don't want to lose her again. Whether she remembers me or not, I don't want to let her go. I can't.

She wakes up the moment I sit her down on the bathroom counter. Her eyes jolt open and she looks slightly panicked, until they land on me. I hold my hands up in mock surrender. I didn't mean to scare her, but it warms my heart when she visibly relaxes when she realizes she was with me.

"The counter is cold. Give a girl some warning next time."

I'm slightly startled by her carefree reaction. I expected some kind of anger from her, but I didn't get any. I start talking before that changes, "Look, before you panic or something let me explain."

She quirks a brow at me, gesturing for me to continue.

"I know this is not what we agreed to do. But you were sleeping and I didn't want to just drop you off like what happened tonight– what we did back in those woods– didn't mean anything. I couldn't drop you off at your apartment like you didn't mean anything. It changes things, Chaos. We don't have to get into all of that right now. Hell, we don't ever have to talk about it at all if you don't want to, but I figured the least I could do was bring you back here, to my house, so you could get cleaned up. Let me clean up the mess I helped make and then cook you dinner. If you want to go back to your apartment after everything is said and done, then I'll take you home. Just... just please let me do this for you."

I wasn't lying about my intentions, but I probably would've said anything to earn a few more hours of her time.

She makes a sound that resembles a sniffle and when I lift her chin to see her face better, tears are running down her cheeks. The panic sets in. I went too far. I already fucked this up.

"What did I do wrong? What did I say? I'm so sorry, I didn't mean to upset you."

She grabs my face and smiles through the tears. "You didn't do anything wrong, Atlas."

My panic lessens at the sound of my name leaving her lips. "Then why are you crying?"

"They're happy tears, you big dummy. No one has ever cared enough to do anything like this for me."

I brush her tears away and nod my head. I don't trust myself to speak right now. I can't tell her someone HAS done this for her before. I can't tell her that, that someone was ME! My eyes begin to sting slightly as I face my back to her to turn on the shower. I'm fucking spiraling and I know it. Will I destroy my own heart trying to earn hers back? I didn't even believe I had one until her.

Once the water is hot enough, I strip off my clothes before turning my attention back to her. She's checking me out, not even trying to be subtle about it. Her cheeks turn pink the moment she realizes I caught her staring. I don't call her out on it, but I can't hide the smirk on my face.

I wedge myself between her spread legs, and place both hands on her knees. My hands skim up her thighs taking the bottom of the shirt with me until they're resting on her soft plump hips. I grip her hips harder than I probably needed to and pull her body flush against me. The gasp that escapes her slightly parted lips makes all blood rush south. My erection presses against her wet center, but it can wait.

This moment isn't about that. This is about making her feel cherished and treating her like she deserves. This is aftercare not foreplay, no matter how badly I'd love to sink myself inside of her right now. I brush a kiss across her nose as I pull a stick from her hair. When she sees it, she laughs. I'd do anything to keep hearing that sound. The only sound I love more is her moaning my name. Shit, I need to keep my head out of the gutters or I'd never survive this shower.

Emily

He raises my arms and lifts the shirt over my head. I catch a glimpse of myself in the mirror before he grabs my hand leading me into the shower. I look like I crawled out of a swamp, my face still plastered with mud and his dried cum. *So embarrassing.* I step into the shower facing away from him, allowing the spray of hot water to wash away the grime. The murky water swirls around our feet before going down the drain.

As more of the mud washes away, it reveals every single mark left on my skin. A scratch here and there from falling down, but it also shows every mark left behind by *him*. Small fingertip sized bruises scattered across my thighs and hips. A tiny little circle marking every time he held me like he never wanted to let go. There's a hickey on my shoulder that I don't remember him putting there.

Most people may not like having their body marked so blatantly but to me, it's so much more than that. Every little blemish he gave me is a reminder of the love he showed me. No matter how fleeting this may be, it's proof someone like him loses control around me. It feels so freaking powerful to unravel a man like him.

His hard length brushes against my lower back as he reaches around me to grab a loofah. I snake my hand behind me, barely getting my fingers wrapped around him when he grabs my wrist stopping me. Turning me to face him, he kisses the inside of my wrist before dropping it and cupping my face so I'll hold eye contact with him.

"We have plenty of time for that later. Right now it's about getting you cleaned and fed. Understand?" His voice leaves no room for argument, but I push anyway.

"If you can't keep up just say so." He smirks and starts washing my body. It's the type of smirk that means trouble.

"Keep being a brat and I'll make you go without it even longer."

"You wouldn't dare." He doesn't respond for a moment as he drops to his knees in front of me kissing the marks he left on my hips and thighs. His lips follow the suds as he uses the loofah to wash away any of the remaining mud from my legs. He kisses the scrape on my knee and calf. His lips brush against the scar near my ankle from the surgery, tracing it with his thumb before standing back up.

I squeeze my eyes shut, bracing for the snide remark that never comes. Trevor would always look at it with disgust. It's part of the reason I normally hide it with high top converse or long socks. But Atlas isn't Trevor.

"Are you willing to bet on it?"

I slap him on his chest and turn away from him reaching for the shampoo. Anything to cover up my reaction.

"Let me do it."

Taking the shampoo from me he squeezes some into his hands before lathering it through my hair. His nails scrape gently as he scrubs my scalp. I rinse out the suds and he grabs the conditioner. He starts applying the conditioner to the ends of my hair and working his way up. Making sure to apply it evenly to my hair before his fingers start moving in a massaging motion on my scalp before detangling the strands with his fingers. He's so good at this, how many other women has he done this for? Am I just the next one in a long line?

"Treat all the women you sleep with like this?" I try to play it off like a joke but I'm not sure it came out that way when he tenses behind me. I don't think I like how that question makes me feel. Like I swallowed lead. Is this what jealousy feels like? I can tell you now I'm not a fan of it. The worst part? I have no right to feel this way. I have no claim on him. We're practically strangers, so why does my stomach get upset every time I think of him with someone else? I forget I even asked him a question until he speaks.

"There are no other women, Chaos. I've only ever done this for you."

The words sound like they almost pain him. They're heavy. They seem to carry more meaning behind them than he intended them to. I drop the conversation, no longer trusting my voice to speak. He continues washing my hair in silence, neither one of us breaking the tension.

It's not awkward, but you can feel the weight it holds. Like what we're doing here means way more to both of us than it should. We don't know each other, yet I feel like he's the only person who I can show the real me. I'm so lost in my own thoughts I don't even notice he has already washed himself until he's reaching around me to shut off the water.

He hands me a fluffy white towel to dry off with, already having one wrapped around his waist, before walking out of the bathroom. Did what I say bother him that badly? Did I mess this up? I dry off as quickly as I can and tiptoe into the bedroom with a towel wrapped around me. Sitting on the bed is one of his black shirts and a pair of black boxer briefs and black socks. I dress quickly and follow the sound to the kitchen where I assume he must've gone to start cooking.

I take in my surroundings as I slide into the bar stool set up against the kitchen island. This kitchen is huge. Honestly I've always dreamed of having a kitchen like this. The fridge looks like pantry doors and he has an espresso machine in the corner sitting on what I could only describe as a coffee bar.

I watch him for a few more moments, not wanting to break the trance he seems to be in. He's shirtless, wearing nothing but grey sweat pants. I laugh to myself. With me in his shirt and briefs, it's almost like I'm wearing the rest of his outfit.This man is so good looking it's not fair. Sculpted back, muscular arms, that v-shape leading your eyes to his waist band. The man was edible, I swear. He seems so focused and so at peace right now. Something in my brain feels a little foggy as I observe him cook with such ease. It's like I'm trying to recall a memory that no longer exists. Shaking the thought away I finally say something.

"Thank you for cooking for me Atlas, you really didn't have to."

"I wanted to, Chaos. It's no big deal, just food."

"Well, can I help you at all?"

"No need, it should be done shortly if you want to go ahead into the living to turn on a movie for us to watch. That would be great."

"Yeah, sounds good. Um... have you seen my phone? I haven't seen it since we...." My cheeks turn pink as I replay the woods in my head. Even though I'm clumsy as hell, I wouldn't mind doing that again one day.

"Yeah, I put it on the coffee table for you. The TV remote should be right next to it. If you need anything before dinner is done just yell."

I nod my head again, making my way over to the big fluffy sectional in his living room. I've never nodded my head so much in my life. I feel like one of those plastic bobble head figures, but it's almost as if I don't trust what I might say around him. The remote and my phone are exactly where he said they'd be. Turning on the TV, I press play on the first comedy movie I scroll across before grabbing my phone and checking my notifications.

Most of the notifications on my phone are just emails or social media notifications that don't matter, so I just swipe away. It's the text message waiting for me that makes me pause.

Trevor: I made it. I won't be gone too long.

Something about this text doesn't sit right. It almost feels ominous but I'm probably just overthinking it. Before I have the chance to decide on a response Atlas clears his throat behind me. I whip my head around like I was caught doing something wrong. He has a plate of food for each of us, but his eyes are locked on my phone screen.

"I didn't mean to intrude. You looked upset or worried so I glanced at your screen, sorry."

"Oh, it's okay..." I say with a smile.

He sits both plates down on the table before sitting on the opposite side of the couch. "I know I should've probably asked before all of this began between us. I was being selfish and wanted to be blissfully unaware of anyone besides us, but do you have a boyfriend I should be worried about?" Any trace of a smile vanishes from my face.

"A boyfriend... no. I would no longer call Trevor that. But it's kind of complicated and hard to explain."

"Do you think you could try? Try to explain it to me so I can understand."

How do I explain Trevor without sounding like I'm stringing Atlas along. Lying won't get me anywhere, not with how Trevor can be, so I tell him the truth. My mouth feels very dry all of a sudden but he deserves to know. Will he leave when he realizes I come with too much baggage?

"I... I've been with him for years. Well at least I was until recently. This is probably going to sound crazy, and if it's too much for you to deal with then I'll understand. I'm sure you've noticed I sometimes have a limp. I had to have surgery. Well, when I woke up in the hospital after the surgery, I had no idea why I needed it in the first place. But it was more than that. I woke up missing almost a year's worth of time."

My eyes start to water as I continue explaining this to him. He doesn't cut me off or say anything, but I feel his warm hand take mine, giving me a reassuring squeeze.

"Th- there are moments where my dreams feel vivid enough that I wake up wondering if they were actually suppressed memories. They always feel too real."

"What's the last thing you remember?"

I pause for a moment to truly think about my answer. "The last thing I remember before waking up in the hospital bed was watching a movie with Trevor. It feels like I blinked and was in that bed. I opened my eyes after surgery with no recollection of all that missing time. So much time just erased from my mind. No one would give me answers- Not Trevor, not the doctors- no one. They said the anesthesia caused the lapse in memories. That it was normal and not to worry about it. But they refused to tell me why I needed the surgery to begin with. I don't know why but something felt off about the entire situation. He took me home to our apartment I didn't even remember having. I told him I needed time away from him, time to recover, but it's almost impossible to avoid someone when his name is on the lease. Hell, if I'm being honest, I don't even remember moving to this town to begin with."

Chapter Seventeen

Atlas

Her confession has me reeling. I don't think I've ever stopped to think about how hard it might be for her to not remember. I couldn't imagine how I'd react to waking up and it all just being gone. Will she hate me if she ever finds out the secrets I'm keeping from her? It takes everything in me not to tell her everything.

The words slip out before I can stop them. "So what now?" Her confusion is evident on her face as her wide eyes lock onto mine.

"What do you mean?"

My heart is pounding in my ears. I'm not sure I'll be able to survive depending on what her answer may be. "After everything you just said, where does that leave us? Where does that leave me?"

" I'm not following..."

"Do you want me in your life, Chaos? Am I just a place holder for you while you figure everything out? I need to know what this is between us and if you plan to go back to Trevor. Save me from myself before I get too invested in something I can't have."

Her hand wraps around my wrist stopping me in my tracks. I didn't even realize I was pacing until she stopped me. "After everything I just said, that's what you're worried about?"

"Yeah. Why?"

"I wouldn't have unloaded all my baggage at your feet if I didn't want something real with you, Atlas. You're standing here asking me what's next when I was panicking thinking you were going to tell me to leave."

"Then stay."

"You don't mean that." I can see in the way that she looks at me she's trying to rebuild every wall I had to break through. She's trying to protect herself from the rejection that'll never come.

"I mean it. Every word. Move in. You can have your own room, your own space, but stay with me. You don't need to stay tied to Trevor if you don't want to. We can figure everything out when we get to it, but let me help."

"Okay," she said it so quietly I almost missed it.

"Wait. What did you just say?"

"I said, okay. I'll move in."

At least I know my ears work. For a moment, I was so sure I imagined her answer. I didn't think she'd agree that easily. Without hearing any of the reasons I prepared for her, she agrees. Not even a full discussion about it. I drop the conversation for the time being. She said okay and for now, that was good enough. We could figure everything else out tomorrow. "We should probably eat even though it's probably cold already."

She laughs, "Yeah. You're probably right."

Emily

We finally get around to eating the food he made for us. It's ice cold but it doesn't matter. I'm starving and it tastes amazing even without it being hot. It looks like some kind of pasta. There are sun dried tomatoes, mushrooms, and sliced chicken in a pinkish orange sauce.

We eat in complete silence, the only sounds being the movie playing in the background and our forks scraping against our plates, but it isn't awkward. It usually isn't now that I think about it. With Atlas, I never feel I have to force a conversation just for the sake of talking. It's like he understood me without me having to tell him.

He asked me to move in and I didn't hesitate. I said okay the minute the question slipped out. I don't need to think about it. It may sound crazy but I knew right away I wanted to be here with him. This feels like home.

The movie ends and I stand to take our plates to the kitchen, rinsing them off before placing them in the dishwasher. When I come back to the living room, he's laying back on the couch pressing play on another movie. He gestures for me to walk to him. I hesitate but eventually, I give in. The moment I'm within reach, his hand wraps around my knee and he pulls me to him. I know he's only trying to get me to lay down on the couch with him, but I pivot and drop to my knees in front of him.

"What do you think you're doing?"

"I'm thanking you for dinner. What does it look like?"

"I didn't cook to get my dick sucked, but you already know that don't you?"

"And if I want to? Are you telling me I can't?" I run my hands up his thighs batting my lashes for a little added flair. He clenches his jaw and the growing tent in his sweatpants is proof enough he wants this just as badly as I do.

I use my index finger to trace the outline of him while my other hand grasps the band on his sweatpants. I flick my eyes to him, waiting to see if he plans to stop me. He doesn't stop me, just gives me a subtle nod to continue.

"Tsk tsk, if you make me use my words, then you have to use yours. A nod just won't do."

I yank his sweats down just far enough to free him, his dick popping free and resting against his belly button. My fingers wrap around him, giving him a light stroke. I circle my tongue around his tip in slow, teasing licks before licking pre-cum from his slit. His skin is as soft as velvet. I kiss his hip before biting hard enough to leave a mark. I want him to look at it and remember me leaving it just like I will for all the marks he left me. I place another kiss at his base. I want to keep pushing until he snaps. Then I lick underneath, following the vein from base to tip. A groan leaves him. His fingers tangle into my hair, yanking my head back far enough that I'm forced to face him as he leans closer to me.

"Keep playing games and I'll tell you no."

A chuckle slips out of my parted lips. "Just be a fucking good boy and-" I don't get to finish my sentence. My words are cut off by his dick being shoved down my throat. I wonder what pushed him over the edge. Was it the *good boy* part?

He fucks my mouth with abandonment and I love every single second of it. I moan and gag around him as he uses my hair to match my pace with his. I knew he was getting close. His movements get sloppier as he swells in my mouth. He thrusts one more time before stilling in the back of my throat. He plugs my nose as he spills his cum forcing me to swallow every drop before allowing me to breathe again.

Chapter Eighteen

Emily

The week I just spent with Atlas was amazing. I felt like I was free to be myself. We swung by my apartment after that first day to grab a bunch of my stuff. I know there are a lot of things I need to take care of soon. Like the apartment I technically share with Trevor. While I know I can't ignore it all and wish it away, I didn't have a plan yet. I need to pack my stuff and remove myself from the lease, but we can figure that out when the time comes. He drove me to work the first two days and I ended up taking the rest of the week off. I knew my time alone with Atlas was running out and I didn't want to waste it.

It only takes one single glance at my notifications for everything around me to shatter. I have four missed calls from Trevor yet he didn't leave a voicemail. If it was important he would've left one right? It's almost like he knows I'm with Atlas. Could he? I feel slightly guilty for being here, but it's not like me and Trevor are still together. I sent him a text to see why he called.

Emily: Hey sorry I missed your call, is everything okay?

> Trevor: I will be back in an hour. I was calling
> to see if you were at work or the apartment.

> Emily: I am off today. I will be at the
> apartment.

Fuck. Fuck. Fuck. I couldn't exactly tell him where I was. I look at Atlas who's smiling until he sees that I'm visibly tense.

"What's wrong?"

"I had four missed calls from Trevor so I texted to see what he wanted.." I hand him my phone so he can read it for himself.

"You're not going."

"I have to Atlas. I need to end it with him once and for all. If I don't, he'll never leave me alone."

"Fine. Okay. Okay. Go to the apartment and meet him. You call me if you need me, then you can meet me back at Pages afterward. Text me when you get there please. I want to give you time to talk, but if you don't text saying you made it or if I don't hear from you within forty minutes, then I'll come to the apartment looking for you."

I beat Trevor to the apartment, he should be here in about ten minutes. I have to try and figure out how to act like everything's normal. I turn on a movie and scroll halfway through it so it looks as if I've been here for a while.

I tense when I hear the front door shut. This is it, don't fucking panic, everything is fine. He waltzes in like he owns the place, which I guess in a way he does. He kisses my forehead before plopping down on the couch next to me.

"What no hello? I thought you would've at least missed me."

"Hey, Trevor. No. It's not like that. I'm a bit tired. How was the trip?"

"It was fine. What are you watching?"

"Just some rom-com. Um.. Can we talk about something?"

"What is it?"

I stand and start pacing before finally saying what I need to say. "I need whatever this is to stop. I already told you I needed time to recover from everything. I appreciate everything you've done for me, but it's not working for me anymore."

He turns to face me and I see his carefully curated smile crack. His face goes completely blank. His eyes look hollow, his voice holds no emotion when he finally speaks. "You think I don't know that you've already been seeing someone else? You're fucking stupid to think I didn't see you sneaking around with him. What's his name? Atlas was it?"

I can feel my panic rising. I didn't think he knew about Atlas. "He's my friend, Trevor. That's all."

"Keep lying through your teeth and fuck it up even more than you already have."

Hearing his words feels like a gut punch. Before I can say something he reacts faster than I expected. I don't even see him move. One moment I'm standing there and the next, my breath is knocked out of me as he slams me against the wall.

He grabs my jaw hard enough to leave a bruise. His body is pinned to mine, keeping me in place as he digs in his pocket for something. This is not the Trevor I remember and not the same man he has been acting like lately.

He must find what he's looking for because he lets out a small chuckle. It lacks any emotion and my stomach sinks to my feet. I already know I'm not going to like what happens next. He yanks my chin away from him, exposing my neck completely.

What the hell is this psycho going to do now?

I open my mouth to question him but my words don't get the chance to form on my tongue. I feel the sharp pinch of a needle before my blood runs cold and everything goes black.

Chapter Nineteen

Atlas

Something about her going to that apartment alone to meet him caused a pit to form in my stomach. Even though I want to stop her from going, I know I can't. This is something she needs to do on her own and I have to respect that. I give her a quick kiss and then I watch her leave. Once she's out of sight, I head back inside to get dressed.

The drive to Pages is quick. I park my Audi on the curb and head inside to the cozy little corner that has become our spot. It shouldn't be too much longer before she's heading this way to meet me.

An hour comes and goes. How long could their conversation last? My anxiety builds with each passing minute. I pull my phone out to make sure she hasn't contacted me asking for help. Nothing. No text or missed calls from her. She definitely should've been here by now. My little stalker is never late which makes me worry even more.

Is she leaving me again? After everything? Is that why she needed to talk to him in person instead of just texting? I try to weigh my options. I need answers, but I don't want to interrupt her if she's fine.

I cave anyway and decide to call her.

It goes straight to voicemail and my world freezes. She wouldn't have turned her phone off. I ran out of the bookstore and jumped in my car.

I crank the car and I'm already speeding towards her apartment before I even have time to put on my seat belt. I click it into place as I take a corner a little too sharp. My tires screech to a halt as I throw the car into park right outside her apartment. I don't even take the time to park in a spot or turn it off before getting out and running to her door.

My stomach sinks as I come up to her door. It's cracked open. I enter the apartment and desperately search for her, but no one is here. The living room looks messed up. Like there was some kind of commotion. I glance around looking for any clues when my eyes land on a syringe on the carpet.

No. No. No. No. This can't be happening right now. I just got her back. This is *not* fair. Life doesn't get to take her from me again.

Gavin picks up on the second ring. "What do you want now, loser?" He said it in a joking manner but I'm in no mood for his shit right now.

"He took her."

"Who took who?"

"Trevor fucking took her Gavin!" I shout as I climb back into the car and speed towards the house.

"Woah, woah, slow down. Tell me exactly what happened."

I retell him everything from today's events when it clicks into place. This is bigger than I thought. "Gavin... you remember a while back when you helped me install that secret tracker but I couldn't tell you why?"

"Yeah... what about it?"

"I was pretty sure Maizyn had a stalker back then. That's why I needed it. Then the car accident. No witnesses but someone dropped her off at the hospital. What if they were the same person? What if it was Trevor this whole time?"

"Shit. That's not impossible. Let me run facial recognition with that hospital photo and his picture to see if it's a match...." After a few tense moments of silence, "Fuck! Atlas it's a match."

"I'm almost to you now. Fucking find him, please. I don't care what it takes, just do it. Call Ramos too if you have to."

I'll stop at nothing to find her. I should've never let her walk out that door alone. I said the same fucking thing last time. You would think I learned from my mistake. She's my entire world and I'll burn this one down if I need to.

Chapter Twenty

Emily

I crack one eye open to take in my surroundings. I might be impulsive but I'm not stupid. If I can assess the situation without alerting anyone that I'm awake, I'll have more time to make a plan. Other than a headache and rope burn from my bound wrist, I feel fine. Good, less injuries will work in my favor. I haven't heard any movement yet, so safe to assume I'm alone for the time being. Opening both eyes fully, I'm able to really look at my situation. I'm tied to a fucking chair in what seems to be an abandon warehouse. Well at least my clothes are still on, that's a plus.

I start wiggling in the chair, testing my restraints and the steadiness of it when I feel it. I can't help but chuckle to myself. Who kidnaps someone, but doesn't check their pockets? *Fucking amateur.* You'd think if he was going to go through all this effort, he'd at least take the knife out of my pocket after he tied me up. Honestly, he never seemed to be that bright.

Not sure why I'm surprised he can't even kidnap someone correctly. Everyone always gave me odd looks when I told them I always have a knife. They said I was paranoid. Who's paranoid now, assholes? I'd rather be prepared in case shit like this happens than not have it when I need it. Trevor must've never paid attention to that fact or he thinks I'm too fucking helpless that he didn't even care.

I stretch my fingers out far enough to reach the cool metal of the switch blade in my pocket. The smooth metal feels right in my grasp, and the distinct click of the blade flipping and locking into place is calming. I take a deep breath as I slowly move the blade so it's wedged between the rope and my wrist. I slowly move the knife up and down against the ropes. A sharp burning pain flairs in my arm where the blade accidentally grazes it.

Fuck that hurt.

They make this shit look easy in books and movies. Well, it's not easy. My arm hurts and blood is trickling down it while I'm barely making a dent in the fibers of the stupid rope. Zero out of ten, do not recommend it. Okay, so the sawing motion is not helping me at all. It's time to think of another tactic.

I place the handle under me so I'm sitting on it with the blade facing away from me, forcing my arms to bend against their will as I manage to place the rope underneath the blade without cutting myself any further. Leaning back, I make sure my weight will hold the blade still enough and pull my wrist upwards with as much force I can muster. The movement feels awkward with my elbows bent at an odd angle, but I'm soon rewarded with the satisfying pop of the ropes snapping. I can actually do this. Hope swelled in my chest but I tried to push it back down. Hope had the power to get you killed. Hope made you sloppy. It made you make poor choices and I planned to make it out of here alive.

I untangle the tattered rope from my arms before leaning over to cut the ropes tying my feet to the chair. It only takes me a few seconds to free each leg. It's so much easier to do when my hands are free. Checking my arms over for injuries reveals the rope burns around both wrists will probably last longer than the small knife nick on the inside of my arm. My ankles were tied over my socks so there's barely even a mark left behind on them.

Not too bad for my first time getting kidnapped.

Now what? So many options. I could leave, but that'd mean he would only try again. It'd be a never ending cycle of looking over my shoulder. It also puts Atlas at risk. No, that just wouldn't do. Hmm, I got it! I'd just give him a taste of his own medicine, but I'll be better at it than he was. I'll beat him at his own sick games. My mind swirls as all the crazy ideas bounce around. I was going to get my revenge. If this happened a few months ago, I probably wouldn't have cared, but now I have something worth fighting for.

My eyes start darting around the room, looking for anything heavy and easy to swing. I wasn't dumb enough to think I could ever over power him without some kind of help. Putting my knife back in my pocket, I start searching around stacks of wooden crates for something that'll help, when I hear what sounds like a car pulling up outside. That has to be him. I don't have much time left. Panic starts to bubble up in my stomach when I finally spot it. Wedged between a crate and a barrel is a big rusty shovel. It'll have to do.

I quickly grab it and dart down behind a stack of pallets close to the door. He'll have to walk past my hiding spot in order to see I'm no longer tied to the chair. That'd give me just enough time to try and knock him out. I would only get one shot at this. I can't afford to mess this up. My heart beat is pounding so loud, I'm terrified he'll be able to hear it. I force myself to take deep, calming breaths and I wait.

I can hear the beep of a keyfob locking the doors on a car and the distinct sound of footsteps stomping through dirt. Good to know wherever we are, it's far enough away from the city to be dirt instead of asphalt– great. I wipe my sweaty palms on my jeans and grip the shovel as tight as I can with both hands. The last thing I need is this stupid shovel slipping from my fingers because my hands were too sweaty.

I take one last deep breath and brace myself as I hear the twist of the door knob. The door opens and he strolls in like he didn't have a care in the world. Like I said, he wasn't that bright. As soon as his back is turned towards me I come out from behind the pallets. I let go of the breath I was holding. Exhaling it in a scream of rage as I swing the shovel as hard as I can. It connects with the back of his head with a solid whack, but it wasn't hard enough.

He stumbles and tries to recover, but before he can, I swing again. This one hit closer to his jaw as he turned to face me. The *ting* sound of the shovel pinging off his skull was slightly satisfying. Watching him crumble into a heap on the floor makes me smile, but my work isn't over yet.

I grab him by the ankles, dragging his heavy body to the chair I was occupying not that long ago. I really need to work out more, or maybe he should have. Maybe he wouldn't weigh so much if he knew what a treadmill was. His dead weight is almost impossible to drag. I'm pouring sweat by the time I get him in front of the chair, and I still have to manage to get him into the freaking thing.

You know what, fuck it. I roll him onto his side and, unlike when he tied me up, I pat him down. Checking his front pockets, I take the cash from his wallet along with his car keys. He won't be needing either. As I go to check his back pockets I see the outline of a gun tucked into his back. Yeah, I'll be taking that. I quickly tuck it into the waist band of my shorts as I retrieve his phone out of his pocket.

Finally happy he won't have any help getting out of this, I slide the chair behind him and line it up so I can tie it to him. Figured it would be easier to tip the chair up with him already attached to it versus the other way around and if not, at least he'd be tied to the chair either way.

I grab some rope and fasten each wrist to the back legs of the chair just below the seat. I pull the knots as tight as I can before I move on to his legs which I tie to the chairs front legs. I then tie some rope around his torso. The less he can move, the better. Once I'm happy with my tie job, I prepare for the hard part, lifting him and this heavy ass chair up. I flip him to where the back of the chair is laying on the ground, then I use all the leg strength I have to lift the chair until the legs are on the floor again.Damn, I really need to work out more– I'm not made to be lifting bodies. I can feel the panic slowly rising. What do I do now? Do I just leave him here? He could slowly starve to death. It's not like he wouldn't deserve it. But that would give him time to escape. Should I call the cops? I could turn him in for kidnapping. Was it still kidnapping if I was a grown woman? Before I'm able to come up with a game plan, Trevor starts to move. Great, I was hoping to be gone before he woke up.

I turn to face him as he groans and shakes his head until he's fully awake. I don't know how he'll react and I don't want to give him the chance to catch me by surprise. He starts yanking on his binds in frustration. You can tell by his rigid posture that he's currently trying to connect the dots of how he ended up this way. He mumbles a curse and I couldn't hold it in anymore, I laughed. It was comical seeing his inflated ego shrink just a little. Sadly he didn't think it was as funny as I did. When his head snapped to where I was standing, he grew even angrier. If looks could kill I'd probably be dead.

Too bad for him they couldn't.

"You're a lot stupider than I gave you credit for, Emily. He already threw you away once, you dumb cunt. You're broken, nothing more than damaged goods. You're lucky I even tried to love you.

He's just using you again. There's no way someone like him will love someone as messed up as you, Emily."

While what he said kind of stung, I knew I was broken. Him saying that wouldn't get him the reaction he hoped for. I've heard something similar my entire life, so it wasn't anything new. But what did he mean by again? Who's he talking about? I really wasn't sure. He's probably just talking out of his ass like he always did.

"You're wrong, Trevor."

"Am I though? How well do you really know him?"

"I know him well enough."

"He's not going to give you the soft and sweet type of love, Emily. No one will. Sluts don't get the happy kind of love where a man's touch will make you shiver in bliss. No one will treat you the way I was willing to. But that wasn't good enough for you was it? You had to go and open your legs for someone else."

"I don't want soft. I don't want lingering glances and sweet kisses. I don't want shivering. I want his touch to fucking burn. I want obsession and devotion. I don't want love that's too simple. I want destruction. I want something I'd rather die than live without. That was never you, Trevor."

"And you think that's him? He sure as hell didn't give you that last time? You don't even know the secrets he has been keeping from you, yet you think he loves you."

"What the hell do you mean by that? Why do you keep saying *'again'* and *'last time'*? What are you hiding?"

"Wouldn't you like to know? But that's okay. When I get out of here, I'll save you the trouble and just kill him. He can't get in my way anymore if he's not breathing. You could've just picked me, but no, you had to go and be a whore. You're such a dumb bitch.

You belong to me, no one else but ME. I'll kill you and him before I let him have you again."

My body shakes with anger as I pull the knife from my pocket and flick it open. Threatening me was one thing, but I wouldn't let him threaten Atlas. He let out a sound that can only be described as a manic cackle.

"What are you going to do with that? Kill me? You don't have what it takes. You're nothing more than a worthless broken doll."

My body moves instantly. The moment he said I didn't have what it takes, was the moment he signed his own death certificate. There's no hesitation as I stab him with the knife. That's when I feel it, the warmth of his blood pouring over my clenched fist that's now holding the knife that's currently plunged in his throat. It's like my brain shuts off, the only voice I hear doesn't sound like mine. It's happy with what I did.

The smell hits me next, a mix of metallic and something that smells an awful lot like piss fills the air. A smile cracks across my lips as I watch him panic. It feels broken and cracked, like it doesn't belong on my face. He's trying to speak, but it comes out in a bloody gurgle. He thrashes against his restraints, getting one of his arms free.

His fingers wrap around my wrist, trying to remove the knife. I push it in further as he claws at my forearms. He's fighting for his life. Not that it'll do him any good at this point. His nails dig in hard enough to break my skin, but it only adds to his blood that already drenches my arms.

"Not so strong now are you, Trevor?" I twist the knife just a little and he thrashes with panic, but he doesn't fight long. His eyes meet mine for a brief second. It's clear the moment he realises he's not getting out of this alive. Several emotions flash in his eyes before they land on regret. His hand drops limply to his side as life finally drains from his body.

I expected to feel terror– regret even– but as I stare at the man I just killed, I no longer feel anything.

Suddenly the warehouse door is thrown open and I let go of the knife handle, quickly drawing the gun stashed in my waist band. I just killed one person. I'll not hesitate to kill another. I'll be getting out of here alive one way or another. My finger twitched on the trigger as the intruder rounded a stack of wooden crates. I pulled the trigger but aimed right next to his head. I know the eyes staring back at me, but why are they here?

Chapter Twenty-One

Atlas

It took me way longer to find her than I wanted to. By the time I tracked down the warehouse, Trevor's car had already been here for fifteen minutes. My stomach drops to my feet as I prepare myself for what I might see here. She's been gone for twenty four hours. I don't even know if she's still alive, but I know either way, Trevor won't be after this. Gavin is in my ear piece but I no longer hear him over the sound of my pounding heart. I know he has a drone in the sky to run thermals and keep an eye out for any trouble, but I don't wait for him to tell me what I'm running into. I already wasted enough time. I draw my gun and throw open the warehouse door.

I duck down when a bullet buzzes right past my head. I go to return fire but stop dead in my tracks. It's not Trevor shooting at me. I'm frozen for a second, my brain trying to catch up to what I'm currently seeing. I came here to rescue her but there's a gun aimed at me, and she's the one holding it.

She's drenched in blood but I can tell it's not hers. I glance around to take in the scene. There doesn't look to be anyone else here, well besides Trevor's dead body. Her knife is still sticking out of his neck as blood continues to pool in a puddle at his feet. Damn, I just missed all the action. She doesn't seem to be in shock or upset over his death either. She looks every bit of the name I gave her. The chaos was palpable. You could feel it in the air– an electric feeling. Like any sudden movement would cause the air to spark. I've never seen her this unhinged.

My dick twitched at the sight of the carnage she unleashed. I don't know what that says about me, but I didn't care to dwell on it. She could shoot me right now and I'd probably smile. She was bathed in his blood and looked like the queen of hell. I'm not exactly happy she had to get her hands dirty, but she made my job easier by taking him out. Now I just had to talk her down so she'd let me take her home.

"Lower the gun, Emily."

"Why the fuck should I?"

"Because I'm not here to hurt you."

"Then why the fuck are you here? How did you find me anyways? Trevor mentioned you were keeping something from me. Are you in on this?"

"I came to save you." Her smile was manic as she put her finger back onto the trigger but pain flickered in her eyes before she masked it. Seeing that look on her face started to unravel me. My composure was starting to slip away.

"Clearly I don't need you to save me. Why would you risk your life to do that anyways? You don't even know me."

"That's where you're wrong, Chaos."

The gun shook in her hands a little, almost like she wasn't sure what to believe before she raised it to my head. "How do I know I can trust you?" Her voice cracked on the last two words and I couldn't hold back anymore. No matter what the fallout will be from this I can't keep the truth from her anymore. She can hate me, but after everything that's happened, she deserves to know.

"Oh Darling Chaos, don't you fucking get it? Haven't you figured it out yet? Those memories you're missing belong to me. You belong to me! You might not remember, but I could never forget. You own my soul, Chaos. Whether you remember that or not! I know I'm in that head of yours somewhere. I see the recognition flicker in your eyes before it vanishes again. It's torture. My heart breaks again every time it fades."

Emily

It's too much. I squeeze my eyes shut to try and block him out but the opposite happens. Memories start flickering behind my closed lids like an old movie projector. Flashes of this man that feel too real to have been figments of my imagination. Too many thoughts and images fight for control. My hands shoot up to cover my ears. The cold metal of the gun barely registers against my warm skin as I press in against my temple. I want it all to stop but it doesn't– Image after image, one memory to the next.

Every single one involves him. All the dreams I was having lately weren't dreams, but memories that were locked away. His voice is bouncing around my psyche like a skipping CD. It's suffocating.

I remember EVERYTHING! I remember the fact I changed my name because I was running from my old life. The fake documents I hired some weird kid to make for me. The night we met at Elixirs flashes in my mind, that time he fucked me on the hood of his car. I remember the way he always looked at me. It was like he was the only one who saw the real me.

I blink and my mind flashes to us arguing.

The night I left replays in my head like I'm reliving it. Along with the memories, comes the flood of emotions that accompany them. Tears are streaming down my face and I don't think they're stopping anytime soon. I'm breaking down bit by bit, unraveling further and further with each new memory unlocking.

I remember leaving the bar. I was so drunk I don't even know how I got into the driver seat without falling. I blink again and the memory flashes to me tossing my phone out the window. Another blink, another memory, this time it's drifting off the road into the small ditch. I relive the taxi ride and the voicemail I left Atlas from the taxi driver's phone. The headlights as I looked up towards the noise. The sound of the wreck replays in my head. It's too much. It's all too fucking much.

Is it possible to drown inside your own head? It feels like a river of shit I didn't remember and I'm trying to swim to the surface, but cinder blocks are chained to my feet weighing me down. The pressure keeps building with nowhere to go, so I do the only thing I can to try to ease it— I SCREAM. I scream with everything I have, until my lungs burn with the need for air.

When the burn becomes too much, I finally give in and inhale. As soon as the air inflates my chest, my body gives up the fight. My knees buckle and the sting as they connect with the concrete hits me, but I'm too trapped inside my head to care.

"Spoon. Spoon. Spoon." I mumble the word over and over again like it has the power to make everything stop. That's what he said right? That I need to say my safe word if it's ever too much?

I'm lost in the panic for what feels like forever but it couldn't have been more than a few minutes when I feel arms wrap around me. He pries the gun from my hand and I hear the distinct sound of it clattering to the floor. That does the trick. I snap out of the panic attack as I begin pushing his arms away. I don't want to be held right now, I don't want to be coddled. I want fucking answers and Trevor is no longer alive to give them to me.

Shit that's right, I killed someone. What's going to happen now? I was so wrapped up in my own head I completely forgot. I look at Trevor's dead body but I still don't feel guilty about it. Honestly, I think I killed him too quickly. He should've suffered more. The idea of actually getting a therapist sounded pretty nice right about now, but then I'd have to admit to my crimes, and I didn't have time for that. Atlas lets go without much of a fight and follows my gaze to Trevor.

"We need to deal with him and get out of here before cops come looking. Let me make a call real fast, then we can try to get you cleaned up."

I nod and look down to see I'm still covered in blood. Damn, I made such a mess. Atlas is trying to talk quietly but I can hear every word.

"Yeah Gavin, I got her. No. Look I can explain everything later but I need you to call Ramos. He has connections. Just tell him I need a clean up and send him my current location. Okay. How much time do I have? Got it. Call me if you see trouble."

He ends the call and walks towards me. He looks stressed and I'm not sure if I blame him. Taking his hoodie off, he tosses it at me. I put it on without any argument and pulled the sleeves down to cover up my blood stained hands. This is the best we'll be able to do in regards to cleaning me up. It's not like there's any water here to wash off and I know we're probably almost out of time.

Atlas heads for the exit and I quietly follow after him. He seems to have a plan and I still want answers. We walk a few blocks before I break the silence.

"Why didn't you just tell me the truth when we met? Why all the games?"

"We don't have time for this. Look, I'll tell you everything when we get to my house."

"Tell me now, Atlas. No more secrets between us. Don't you think we had enough of that? I want fucking answers and I'm not going anywhere until I get them."

"Would you have believed me? If I told you the day we met, about everything that happened between us? You would've thought I was crazy. You didn't remember me, I didn't want to force anything on you. I didn't deserve to get you back that way. After what I did, I needed to grovel. I couldn't force you to love me again. You deserved so much better than that. If I'm being honest, you deserved so much better than me. Hell you still do. But... I figured if I could get you to love me again, without me telling you anything about our past, then I earned it. Loving me had to be your choice, and I would've respected your choice no matter what it was. If you would've told me to leave you alone or brushed me off, I would've respected that, no matter how much it wrecked me. I would've let you go if that was what you decided. If that's what you still decide... You could've pulled the fucking trigger back there and shot me, and I wouldn't have stopped you."

"I almost pulled the trigger, Atlas! You could've died and it would've been my fault."

"I would have let you."

"You can't just say shit like that, Atlas!"

"It's the truth. If you decided that was the way I would leave this world, I would've died with a smile."

Th- that's crazy. I don't even know how to respond to that... Why are you even here? You don't NEED Me! You said it yourself the day I left. So why even tell me the truth? Why come after me?"

"This is different, Maze."

That name on his lips stings. It may have been a fake name, but to me that was the realest version of myself. While the name wasn't real, the way I acted was. I didn't hold back or try to be something I wasn't.

"That's not a good enough answer, Atlas."

He looked like he was debating his next answer. When he looks at me, I see it. It's a look only I seem to provoke. He's battling for control of his thoughts, of this moment, and he's losing.

As he steps forward I step backwards until my back is against the wall. Both of his arms come up caging me in and he leans down so we are eye to eye, but he doesn't stop there. He closes the distance between us pressing his forehead gently to mine leaving me no choice but to maintain eye contact with him. His breath brushes against my lips as he speaks, his voice so low I almost miss it even though we're standing this close.

"Because I know what it feels like to lose you for good. I know how it feels to think you're dead and that I'm the reason for it. I know what it feels like to have you own my soul when I wasn't aware I still had one. For months, I replayed the argument in my fucking head over and over again, wishing I was man enough to stop you from leaving. I couldn't escape you even in my sleep. I dreamed about every happy memory we had, just to wake back up to the nightmare I had to call reality. It took fucking losing you to realize you were it for me. You're my fucking *yellow* Maze. The only bright thing in my life. The only person worth losing control for. I'll never let what happened before happen again because I know what my life is like without you, and it's not worth living unless you're in it."

I closed my eyes to prepare myself to respond but when I opened my eyes again, he was gone. What in the actual fuck just happened? I spin around trying to find him but I don't spot him anywhere. How can he say all of that and just walk off?

I slide down the brick wall behind me. I feel my already bloody, skinned knees split back open, but the sting of my split knees feel like nothing in comparison to the way it feels knowing he just walked away. My body goes numb as I go to war with myself. No matter what I try to say to convince myself I'm good enough for someone to love me, the past seems to repeat itself.

He just detonated a bomb. Shattering my whole life, and he walks away like it meant nothing. I curl around myself and try to hold together any part of me I can while I fall apart on this side walk. More memories of the last year flash through my mind and I don't know if I'm going to survive them. I'm starting to think not knowing was a blessing.

I know I am spiraling out again. I squeeze my eyes shut and cover my ears, but it does nothing to quiet all the noise. You can't block out the voices if they're inside your head. Every doubt and fear is being chanted back at me. The worst part, it's not just my voice saying them anymore. I can deal with my own voice telling me I'm worthless, but when his voice joins the chaos, I crumble further inside my own head.

It's his voice telling me I'm too much. That he doesn't need me. That all I do is fuck up his life. I remember the way it felt feeling my heart break in his office that night. He let me leave. If I thought I was broken before, I don't know if I'll survive losing him again. That wreck should've killed me. It would've been easier to deal with.

You know what– Fuck that! He doesn't get to make me fall in love with him again and fucking leave! He doesn't get to make me manic and avoid the fallout. He did this. All of this is his fucking fault. He's the reason I left the first time and he's the reason I'm drowning now. He doesn't get to be a coward this time. If he wants to wreck me, then I'm going to destroy him too. If I lose myself to this, I'm taking him with me.

Chapter Twenty-Two

Atlas

The walk home felt longer than it was. I should've driven home from the warehouse, maybe I could've avoided all of this. The further I walked away from her, the heavier the sinking feeling in my stomach got. I didn't mean to tell her any of that, but I panicked and the moment I opened my mouth it all spewed out like word vomit. All this time keeping everything to myself and I crumble the moment she asks me about it. I wasn't ready to face the consequences. She closed her eyes and I ran. I didn't want to look into them while I watched the love she had for me fade. I'd rather she had shot and killed me back at that warehouse than watch her leave again, so I left before she could. I knew there was no way she'd pick to stay with me after everything I just revealed to her. I don't deserve her and she's smart enough to know that.

I'm pacing my room, attempting to pack a bag but my thoughts are all over the place. I can't stay here without her. It'll also kill me to leave. None of the solutions I come up with seem to be good enough. My steps falter when there's pounding at the door.

Who'd be pounding like that on my door right now? Whoever it is, I just hope it isn't the cops. Storming to the front door, I sling it open without checking the peep hole first. My temper was already boiling over at the fact that this person interrupted my downward spiral. I wanted to self-destruct in peace.

It definitely wasn't the cops. No. On my door step stands my Darling Chaos in all of her glory. She's freshly showered and dressed to destroy anyone who stands in her way. Her hair is still wet and hanging in waves down her back. She's dressed in a plain black cropped shirt with a black and white plaid skater skirt. She paired the outfit with a pair of black high top converse. The green of her eyes is so bright, they look like they're on fire. I swear I can visibly see the chaos and anger currently swirling in them and even though it's aimed at me, she's breathtaking. Her emotions are palpable. The air between us is charged with them. My lips part as if I have any idea what to say to her, but she cuts me off.

"You don't get to say that shit and fucking leave, Atlas! You destroyed my entire world and then walked away like it didn't matter. Like I didn't fucking matter!"

The pain in her voice hurts because I know I'm the person who put it there, but I'm not ready for this conversation. I'm not ready for her to hate me. "I can't do this right now. Just…just take time to think about everything and we can talk about it another time."

"I want to talk now, Atlas. I need answers."

"You don't know what you need right now. Just go."

"Fuck that! I'm not going anywhere until we talk about this. You can't… Why'd you tell me all of that and then just fucking leave?"

"I was scared! Are you happy now? I was scared!"

"You don't get to push me away just because you're scared. How about you grow a pair and stop being a coward."

"What did you just call me?" She rolled her eyes before her smirk turned crazed. She looks at me like she's about to dump gasoline on the entire situation.

"What? Your ears stop working? Pretty sure you heard me the first time, pretty boy. I called you a coward. Am I wro-" My lips crash against hers, cutting off whatever else she was about to say. As frustrating as it is to admit, she's right. I'm a coward but there's something I want before it's too late. Her.

Emily

The words die in my throat, cut off by his lips on mine. It's intoxicating. He's not sweet or gentle. The kiss is destruction and devastation. It's soul shattering yet not enough. I want answers to every question screaming in my head. Pulling back from him, I break the kiss.

"Why?"

He shakes his head from side to side as he pulls me closer to his body and shuts the door behind us. I was so focused on him, I completely forgot we were standing in his doorway.

"Can you just stop asking for answers right now?"

"No." My answer is blunt but the fact that he's still dodging my questions is starting to annoy me.

"You were just kidnapped. Stop being a damn brat for one second and let me enjoy the fact I have you in my arms before you leave again."

He's crazy if he thinks I'm going anywhere after all of this, but I don't tell him that and I'm not giving up that easily. "Make me. Make it worth it or start talking."

The next thing I know, my feet are off the ground and in the air. This motherfucker flips me upside down as if I weighed nothing.

It's like he thinks he's some male entertainer or some shit– such an asshole. My hands shoot to grab his waist to brace myself. This takes 'face down ass up' to an entirely new level. My thighs are over his shoulders with feet in the air crossed behind his head. I'm eye level with the tent in his pants. My skirt flips up revealing my ass to him. One of his hands is digging into my hip to keep me in place. If this is how he wants to play then fine.

I move my mouth closer to him and bite him through his jeans– not hard enough to hurt him– but the hiss that escapes makes liquid pool at my center, so I bite him again. His other hand comes down in a heavy smack against my left cheek, and his teeth sink into my thigh just below the apex. Based on the sting radiating from where his mouth is, I already know it's going to leave a bruise if it doesn't break the skin. Good. I loved having his marks on my body.

"Now do as you're told or I won't be so nice next time." My smart remark escapes as a gasp on my lips as he licks me through the thin fabric separating his tongue from my center.

"Undo my belt for me, Chaos. Be a good girl and pull me out before I'm left with a zipper imprint on my dick because of you." His words of praise melt my bratty attitude enough that I'm willing to do as I'm told, my body humming with anticipation. I pull his dick free and it bobs against my lips. I keep my mouth close to him. Close enough that when I wet my lips, my tongue flicks across the salty bead of precum already leaking from his tip.

"Stop being a fucking tease and open that bratty little mouth. Put me where I belong. You can't run your mouth if it's full," His hand lets go of my hip and tangles in my hair. He pulls my head back fair enough to make me open my mouth in a low moan before he shoves my head down on him, until he's filling my mouth completely. He removes his hand from my hair long enough to pull my panties to the side before returning. Tangling his fingers into my hair at the nape of my neck he uses his hold on my hair to set my pace, dragging my mouth up and down his length as he blows cold air against me.

"Already so wet for me," I moan around him as he begins to suck and lap at my clit. He's deliberately teasing me, working me closer and closer to my release without letting me go over the edge. "Make me cum and I'll finally let you finish. If you swallow every drop, then we can have that conversation you wanted."

I hollow my cheeks, sucking a licking with complete abandonment. I'm not sure what pushed me more; the thought of getting to finish or finally getting the answers I wanted. I swallowed around him, gagging slightly on his length. The harder I worked, the faster he did. He matched my pace, his mouth and fingers working more and more moans out of me. The moment his salty taste hits my tongue, I detonate. My thighs squeeze around his head as I suck him dry, swallowing every last drop. Once we were both completely spent, he plopped me down on his couch before collapsing right beside me.

"What do you want to know first?"

Straight to it. At least he kept his word about talking after. I can also admit I'm not as angry as I was when I first arrived, so I ask my first question. The one question that started it all. "Why did you place a tracker on my phone and why didn't you stop me from leaving?"

"I didn't tell you at the time because I didn't want to scare you, but I was pretty sure someone was stalking you. There were threatening letters I found and destroyed before you saw them. I thought the tracker would be an extra layer of protection in case anything happened. After everything that's happened, I'm pretty sure Trevor was your stalker, and I think he caused the accident. I didn't stop you from leaving because I was a selfish prick and didn't think you'd actually leave. Not really at least."

"I mean that makes sense. I ran knowing there was a chance he'd chase after me. I think I used to love Trevor, but now that I reflect on it, I think I was just hoping I'd one day be enough for him to love me. We were young when we met. I did whatever he asked because I thought that's what love was. He told me what to wear and how to act, and for a while, that was okay. It wasn't until five or six years later I realized I was the only one compromising. It was always what he wanted and when he wanted it. He wasn't physical with me, ever, but my mental health started draining. I didn't know how to end it without pushing him over the edge or having him guilt trip me into staying, so I ran. As soon as I had the fake documents made up, I packed a small bag and I left in the middle of the night. I wanted to start over. I thought a new name meant I could actually be myself. I knew he'd come looking for me. He acted like he owned me. Like I was his property. I figured a new name would also let me hide from him."

"Do you have any other questions?"

"Honestly, none that really matter. I think you said most of it earlier."

"Can I ask a few then?"

"Sure. What do you want to know?"

"What happened the night you met me? Why me of all people?"

A smile twitches on my lips. "On my first night away from him, I decided I was going to dress how I wanted for the very first time and I went to a bar. I felt your eyes on me and it felt like you were the first person in my entire life to actually look and see the real me. You didn't look at me like I didn't belong there. You looked at me like I was the only person in the room. You made me want to be bold, so I let my body take over and I ignored every single thought telling me to leave."

"Do you regret ever meeting me? After everything that's happened?"

"No, Atlas. I could never regret meeting you. I'd relive it all again if it means you'll still look at me like this."

"Like what?"

"Like I'm not broken. You look at me like I'm the only person in the room. You look at me like you love me..."

"You're far from broken. You're the strongest person I know. And yeah, when my eyes land on you, no one else matters. My skin prickles whenever you enter the same room I'm in. I could never not see you," He grabs my chin tilting my face up so my eyes meet his. "Of course I love you. It'd be impossible not to. You're my *yellow*, Chaos. I didn't even know what that meant when you first said it, but I think you always have been."

"You're my *yellow* too, Atlas. Always will be." His movement falters before I visibly see his sigh of relief.

"Does that mean you're not leaving again?"

"Leaving was never an option. Look at what happened last time I tried. You're stuck with me now, Atlas." He chuckles at that before finally letting go of my chin.

"So Chaos, what do I call you now? Emily or Maizyn? As long as you're mine, I'll call you whatever you want."

"I was never myself when I was Emily. It always felt like I was pretending to be something I wasn't. I think the first time I ever felt like myself was when I was Maizyn. Emily was who Trevor wanted me to be and I feel like I killed Emily when I killed him."

"Then Maizyn it is. For real this time. We'll do a legal name change and make it real. Are you ready to go?"

"Go where?"

"Back to where everything started."

Acknowledgments

I just want to start out by saying, holy crap, I actually wrote a book. I have always loved writing but never thought I would be able to do something as crazy as this. I just want to thank anyone who has supported me in any way. The fact that people are buying and reading this is beyond mind-blowing.

Thank you to my amazing husband, who has supported me every step of the way. You have been my *yellow* since the day that I met you. You **never** made me feel like I was too much. I wrote almost 60,000 words in this book, yet I still can't find the words to describe how much I love you. We were written in the Cosmos. Thank you for supporting my crazy book habit as well. Oh, one more thing. JUMP. GO. WHERE.

I also want to thank my mom for always supporting my little bookish heart while I was growing up. I wouldn't be the writer I am today without you.

Thank you to my Alpha/Beta Readers Ivette, Seraphine, Niki, Heather, Sarah, Ares, and Tabitha. Your feedback was so helpful in bringing this book together. Your reactions made me laugh and cry happy tears.

To Rachel, having you as my PA has been amazing. You have helped keep me on track and have become my friend in real life. You know my ideas and projects long before anyone else does and I am so excited for what we do next.

To K.R.Ruth, this book would have never started without you. Not only did you push me to start my bookstagram journey in general, but you also encouraged me to begin my writing journey. You helped me in my early plotting stages and gave me the courage to bring this book to life.

Thank you to SB. I appreciate you always answering my random out-of-context questions. Your help has made this journey so much easier for me, and I will forever be grateful. Fair warning, I plan to continue bugging you in the future. LOL

To my ARC readers, thank you for taking a chance on me and my debut book. It means so much to me that you took the time to read and review my first book. I hope you enjoyed it and will continue to read my work.

Enjoy the book?

If you liked the book it would mean so much to me if you took the time to rate and review it on Amazon and Goodreads. If you would like to stay up to date on my next book please follow me on my social media platforms.